PRAISE

MW00426363

"A beautiful story of **forgiveness and love**." —*Reviewer, An Amish Rumspringa*

"Like Amish **soup for your soul**." —*Reviewer, Amish Neighbors*

"Tattie Maggard's characters grow in their faith while struggling with **realistic human struggles**. I recommend this book to those who enjoy Amish fiction." —*Thomas Nye, Author of Amish Park, review for Forbidden Amish Love*

"Very positive, **uplifting** books. I really like this author!" —*Reviewer, The Amish of Swan Creek*

"I think Tattie Maggard might be my **new favorite author.**" —*Amazon Top 50 Reviewer, The Amish Flower Shop*

"...a **charming** Christmas story that will warm the heart." —*Emily-Jane Hills Orford for Readers' Favorite, I Hear Christmas*

"I sure do enjoy reading Ms Tattie Maggard's stories, I'm an old softy and I find myself **crying and laughing at the same time,** my wife thinks I've lost it. Just please keep writing." —*Reviewer, A Christmas Courtship*

WHAT HAPPENS IN ASHEVILLE

AN AMISH RUMSPRINGA BOOK 1

TATTIE MAGGARD

FIVE PORCHES PRESS

Copyright © 2017 by Tattie Maggard. All rights reserved. No part of this publication may be reproduced, stored in a retrieval system or transmitted in any form or by any means without the prior permission in writing of the publisher, nor be circulated in writing of any publisher, nor be otherwise circulated in any form of binding or cover other than that in which it is published without a similar condition including this condition, being imposed on the subsequent purchaser. All characters appearing in this work are fictitious. Any resemblance to real persons, living or dead, is purely coincidental. All scriptures taken from the King James Version of the Bible unless otherwise indicated. Rights to the King James Bible in the United Kingdom are vested in the Crown and administered by Cambridge University Press, the Crown's patentee.

AN AMISH RUMSPRINGA

What Happens In Asheville
Stays In Asheville
Finding Love In Asheville

Sign up for email updates at:
www.TattieMaggard.com

"Behold the fowls of the air: for they sow not, neither do they reap, nor gather into barns; yet your heavenly Father feedeth them. Are ye not much better than they?"
Matthew 6:26 KJV

T welve-year-old Elizabeth Shetler lay in the cool grass on her belly, almost as still as the glossy black crow before her. Its eyes, the same color as its large body, shone with intelligence. It let out a loud "caw" and two more crows appeared in the corner of Elizabeth's eye. She refused to move, even to blink.

He must finally trust me to call in his friends like that.

She fought the urge to squeal. She'd been feeding them handfuls of grain and watching them get closer each time for weeks now. One day she'd touch one.

The crow cocked its head to the side, giving Elizabeth a sharp look, almost causing her to break her stillness. Had he read her mind? She doubted he was that smart, but still, the books and magazines she'd read about birds weren't all correct. She'd read everything her school library had about birds and some of the information had changed from the ones written a long time ago. She'd give anything to go into town to the Asheville library. She wondered how accurate the newer books were.

The bald eagle for instance, who she often saw visit the

1

banks of Swan Creek, wasn't even on the current maps as traveling this far west into Missouri. Was it possible for her to discover something new about the birds she loved that no one else knew?

Respect for her feathered friends went way back. She remembered her *mueter* feeding the hummingbirds every summer from a bright-red plastic feeder she hung from the porch. *Mah* used to let her stir the sugar-water until the tiny crystals were fully dissolved. Then they'd hang it up and wait for the miniature green birds with red-jeweled throats to appear with a hum and happy clicks. *Mah* had taught her how to tell the boys from the girls. Only the boy birds had a red throat. The girl birds were plain—like Elizabeth.

She wished *Dah* would let her put the feeder back up. She had read how the birds returned to the exact same place each year. Perhaps one of them had even known *Mah*.

Elizabeth's eyes stung. She blinked before she could help it. The crow took a little hop forward, never taking his eyes off Elizabeth, and pecked at a piece of grain. From this distance she could make out the teeny feathers by the crow's strong beak. If he ever pecked her it would surely hurt. He was so large, but she wasn't afraid—not the least little bit. Should she dare to move a little closer, or let him come to her?

"So you're the thief!" *Vater's* voice boomed behind her. Elizabeth drew in a sharp breath and squinted her eyes as the birds took flight around her with forceful flaps of their mighty wings. She jumped to her feet, almost tripping on the hem of her dress. She stumbled a step, now looking up into her *vater's* reddened face. The crows soared above the house behind *Dah* and out of sight. Elizabeth wished she could do the same. She braced herself for what would come next.

2

"All this time I thought we had a coon or some other critter eating away at the chicken feed and it was you!" He raised his arm in the air and Elizabeth instinctively put her hands up and closed her eyes tight.

Whap!

It stung instantly. She wondered how the back of his hand could rattle her teeth so. They felt almost numb. She held back the tears, knowing they would only make matters worse. She needed to stay perfectly still until he'd had his say. Only then would he walk away and soon act like nothing had happened.

"Look at me," he barked.

Elizabeth uncovered her eyes, her mouth tightly closed, desperately trying to keep her bottom lip from quivering. His nostrils flared as his breath went in and out. It reminded her of the bull they had in the field. She imagined what her *vater* would look like scratching up the ground like the bull did with one hoof. It would have been a funny picture if she weren't the one he was so mad at.

Why was she the only one he ever hit? Her little sisters could annoy him something awful, make messes all over the place, and even neglect their chores and still not get backhanded. She supposed it came with being the oldest, that and not having *Mah* around, although she could never understand why that made all the difference. But she knew it had. He'd never laid a hand on her while *Mah* was alive.

"Say somethin'," he yelled. But Elizabeth knew better than that. The last time he told her to say something, and she did, he'd hit her again and sent her to bed without supper. The same supper she'd cooked for him! No sir, she would take her chances with remaining silent.

He shook his head forcefully and raised his hand again. Elizabeth closed her eyes, but after a few seconds passed she opened them to find him stomping into the house. Maybe she'd been lucky and he was in a not-so-bad mood. She turned to the spot where the chicken feed lay on the ground and wiped her eyes with the sleeve of her dress, glad the ordeal was over.

She would do it again. It didn't matter how well she obeyed. His moods determined his actions, not her behavior. It had taken her the past year to figure that out. She'd worked too hard to stop now. In a few days, maybe even tomorrow, that crow would eat from her hand—she just knew it.

Elizabeth sniffled and then smiled as the crows began to reappear close to her feet, taking up more grain in their beaks. They hopped around happily in circles. It was as if they were saying *thank you,* or maybe, *we're sorry for the trouble we caused you.*

"You're welcome," Elizabeth whispered so quietly even she could barely hear.

"Get outta' the way, *doomkupf!*" *Vater* shouted.

She gasped with a jump, turning around to find him standing between her and the house with his shotgun in hand. "No, *Dah!* Don't," she cried.

He raised the gun, pointing it in her direction. Would he shoot his own daughter? Elizabeth ran to the outhouse as fast as she could go, not turning around as she heard the shots ring out.

She locked the outhouse door behind her, holding her ears tight. She would never visit that spot again, nor would she ever try to befriend another bird.

CHAPTER ONE

Elizabeth watched as Rebecca Christener made eyes at John Miller. It wasn't often Elizabeth got to stay for a Sunday singing, usually only when church services were held close enough to her home that she could walk the distance. The cooler months would be here soon and she wondered how many singings she'd be able to attend this year. Her *vater* took her and her two younger sisters to every service, held every other week, but when it came to staying to socialize, or coming back to pick Elizabeth up, it was out of the question. She was eighteen years old and he had treated her like garbage ever since her *mueter* died, making Elizabeth wonder why he didn't make the effort to get her married off so he could be rid of her for good.

Lydia, her fifteen-year-old sister, didn't put up with his moodiness and he knew it. Why Lydia was hardly ever on the receiving end of her *vater's* wrath, Elizabeth would never know. Either way, Lydia was old enough to take care of their youngest sister, Anna, and all the chores around the house. Elizabeth had kept up with all of it since she was eleven. It was someone else's turn. Before long, Lydia would start going to the same singings Elizabeth was attending.

Lydia was much prettier with hair the color of chocolate and beautiful brown eyes to match. Elizabeth's hair was blonde and her blue eyes dull and uninteresting, her face small and round with a thin nose that made her look younger than she actually was. Elizabeth was sure her sister would be married off in no time, but it simply wouldn't do for Lydia to marry first. And now Elizabeth had to compete with Rebecca Christener for John's attention while she was trying to have a conversation with him.

Elizabeth was usually too shy to even speak to the young men, much less flirt with them like Rebecca did, but tonight she was feeling rather bold and had engaged John in a discussion about the pros and cons of orange reflector triangles on the back of their topless buggies. How the topic had even come about Elizabeth couldn't remember.

"You're so right, John," Rebecca said as she batted her eyes at him. She had appeared only a moment ago, pushing her way into the conversation where they all stood in the dark barnyard. The gas-powered lights from the open barn doors allowed Elizabeth to see the nearly seductive look Rebecca was giving him.

"Um, I am?" he asked dim-wittedly.

"Sure, I find your views just...fascinating," she said, grabbing him by the arm.

His eyes opened wider and a slow, crooked grin followed. "You do?"

Elizabeth rolled her eyes. He'd only said he thought the bright orange color attracted so much attention that it had to be considered prideful, a view held by about half of the community over the age of fifty. It was hardly an original thought on the matter.

"If you'll excuse me," Elizabeth said out of politeness. She was sure John was too busy to notice her walking away, but at least she had made the effort.

At the refreshment table, Elizabeth took a cookie and a cup of sweet tea. She wondered when she should start walking home. It was apparent she wasn't going to be asked if she needed a ride from any available young man and she wasn't interested in catching a ride with another couple. The walk would take her nearly an hour.

"We just need a couple more people," she overheard someone say from inside the barn. She took a bite of her cookie and strolled in the direction of the voice, the comforting smell of hay greeting her warmly.

"Why do we need anyone else? Isn't three plenty?" another asked.

"*Nay*, you *doomkupf*, we'll have to pay rent somehow. And if we spend all our money on that, how will we have any left to have fun with?" It was Pete and James Wittmer. It wasn't the first time Elizabeth had heard Pete call his brother a *dumb head*. Beside them on the benches still set up for the singing sat Nathan Graber, and so far there were no girls to be seen.

This might be the place to get a ride home.

They stopped talking as Elizabeth approached, and made eye contact. The tension almost brought her to a full stop. They eyed her curiously. She couldn't just turn around and walk off now, even if she wanted to. They knew she had been listening.

"What are you fellas talking about?" she asked, finishing the last bite of her cookie before wiping the crumbs off her fingers onto her dress.

"Nothin'." Nathan smiled slyly.

"We're movin' to Asheville for a while," James said

loudly. Pete slapped him on the back of the head, knocking his black, felt Sunday hat onto the barn floor.

"Asheville? For how long?" she asked, grasping her cup with both hands.

James picked up his hat and dusted it off.

Pete cleared his throat and gave a pointed look toward Nathan.

"Um, as long as need be," Nathan said, seemingly careful to guard his words, his brown hair matching his hazel eyes.

"You're going out on *Rumspringa?*"

He sighed. "*Ja,* but will you keep it to yourself until we're gone? We don't need everyone knowing our business, you know?" Nathan's voice was soft, kind even.

"Of course," she said without thinking. "But wait, you said you needed a couple more people, right?"

"Well..." Nathan shook his head.

James's face lit up. "Yeah, you want to come?"

"Sure," Elizabeth surprised herself by saying. She stopped, her heart beginning to pound. Had she really just agreed to live in Asheville with a bunch of men?

"*Nay,* Elizabeth. You should just stay home." Nathan stood up and leaned against the back of the bench in front of them.

His rejection stung. "Why?" she asked. *Rumspringa* was a time for each of the youth to experience what the world had to offer before they decided whether they wished to join church or not, forever sealing their decision to abide by the *Ordnung,* an unwritten set of rules governing the community.

"This isn't going to be a trip for nice girls," Pete said when Nathan didn't answer immediately.

"What's that supposed to mean?" James asked. "I

thought you said we were going to meet lots of girls on this trip."

"Yeah, *doomkupf*, non-Amish girls," Pete said between gritted teeth. He tried to smack James on the head again but his brother ducked just in time.

"I don't care if they're Amish or not, as long as they're pretty." James winked at Elizabeth. It was a very forward thing for him or any of the male youth to do.

Elizabeth wondered how wild they would get living in Asheville. It wasn't often that anyone actually moved away for *Rumspringa*. She'd heard stories though, from her cousin in Indiana, about how out-of-hand some of the youth had been there. Late night parties with drinking, gambling, guys pairing up with the girls in the dark—nothing she wanted to be involved with, but still—it had to be better than home.

Overcome with sudden courage she said, "I'd love to go. When do we leave?"

"Week from tomorrow," James said.

"Now, hold on a minute," Nathan interrupted. "We're not taking everyone."

"But you said—"

"I know what I said and I think you should stay here. Won't your *vater* need you at home?"

Her *vater*. He'd convinced everyone around that he was just as righteous as anyone by quoting scripture all the time. She supposed he'd convinced Nathan as well.

If only he knew. Elizabeth's jaw clenched tight.

"Hadn't thought about that, had you?" Nathan smiled. "Now, you just keep this between us and I'll see if I can bring you back some trinket from Asheville, all right? I doubt we'll be gone more than a few months."

Tension radiated through her neck to her shoulders at his remark. She wasn't a child, but what could she say? She

9

couldn't get down on her hands and knees and beg, even though the impulse was there. Nodding, she turned to go, kicking herself for not knowing anything else she could do to convince him.

"What'd you go and do that for?" James asked as she began to walk away.

Elizabeth hung her head with a heavy breath as she ambled along. Then her eyes narrowed at the dark ground. If they could go out into the world, why couldn't she? Up until now she'd thought her only way out of her *vater's* house was to marry. But why *couldn't* she just go out on *Rumspringa* and not come back? If James and Pete and Nathan could do it, she could too.

Couldn't she?

But Nathan surely had money put away from the land he'd been farming that his *dah* had given him years ago. And they were all three big, strong men who knew how to do a good day's work. What did she have to offer in the way of skills? Cooking and cleaning? Who would pay for that? She finished her cup of tea and headed for the road.

Nay. If she went out into the world by herself she may very well starve. Still, it was tempting to take her chances. She pondered it on the long walk home.

An hour later, she slipped into the kitchen as silent as a mouse, hoping not to wake anyone. She tiptoed up the stairs of their two-story house and into her bedroom, closing the door behind her. She took off her black *kapp* and let her hair down, then removed her apron and dress, leaving on her old slip to sleep in. Then she pulled down the covers and started to get in her bed when she felt something, or rather, *someone.*

She gasped.

The figure rolled over, "Is it mornin' already?"

Elizabeth slapped at her sister's side. "You nearly scared me to death! What's the matter with you?"

"Sorry," Lydia mumbled.

"What are you doing in here?"

"I just wanted to wait up so you could tell me all about the singin'."

"Couldn't it wait for morning?" Elizabeth lit a lantern on her bedside table, the fumes from the initial light giving off a slight kerosene smell to the otherwise odorless lamp oil. The little flame soon glowed brightly, illuminating the whole room.

Her sister's face was expectant. "*Nay?*" she said with a tiny voice and a scrunched up nose.

"Oh, all right. What do you want to know? And make it quick. I have to be up before dawn to get everyone breakfast and a girl's got to sleep sometime, you know."

Lydia scooted over to make room and Elizabeth slipped under the covers.

"Well, what was the food like?" she asked dreamily.

Elizabeth's mouth dropped open. "You mean to tell me you waited up and nearly gave me a heart attack to ask what kind of snacks there were at the singin'?"

She nudged Elizabeth in the arm. "I just wanted to get a sense of what it was like to really be there."

Elizabeth rolled her eyes.

"I saw that," her sister said. "Fine, just tell me the important stuff, then."

"Like?"

"Like what boys were there!" she said a little too loudly.

"Will you keep your voice down?" Elizabeth whispered angrily. "You know *Dah* doesn't want to be woke up by a couple of giggly girls in the middle of the night."

"I'm sorry. Just tell me something. Anything. I want to

go to a singing so bad I can hardly stand it." Lydia's feet moved around anxiously as she spoke.

Elizabeth sighed. "Well, I did learn something interesting, but you can't tell a soul what I'm about to tell you. I promised I wouldn't be the one to let this get out, but I know I can trust you."

"I promise, I promise."

"A few of the youth—three men I'll not identify by name—are leaving next week to live in Asheville for *Rumspringa*. One of them asked me if I wanted to come." It wasn't exactly a lie. James had asked her and she would have went, too—in a heartbeat—if Nathan hadn't told her she couldn't. He seemed to be the leader of the group. Perhaps it was his idea to leave in the first place.

"And?"

"And what?"

"Are you going?"

"What? *Nay*. I couldn't go. Who would take care of Anna?" Elizabeth held her breath for Lydia's reply.

"Well, I would, silly."

"You?" She tried to sound surprised but it was the answer she had hoped for.

"*Vater's* way too hard on you, but he's not that way with me and Anna. It might do him some *guete* to have time to actually miss you for a while."

Elizabeth sighed. Lydia was fooling herself if she really believed *Dah* would miss her if she left. Could she not see what her *vater* had for her was closer to hate than anything else? If Lydia or Anna left it would be another story. He'd miss them. *Nay*, if she left, she may never be allowed back in the house. She was glad that Lydia was suggesting it, though. At least if she did ever manage to leave, she wouldn't have to feel like she'd abandoned her sisters to do so.

She wondered if the whole house wouldn't be more peaceful with her gone from it. Was she a contrary *doomkupf* like *Dah* always said? Was it her fault he treated her this way? Maybe that's why the *Rumspringa* group didn't want her company.

Was she that hard to be around?

A few minutes later, Elizabeth struggled to hold her eyes open and put out the lantern, before drifting far away in her sleep.

〜

B efore daylight, Elizabeth was up to start chores. The smell of coffee and bacon filled the kitchen before the sun's rays even shone through the window above the sink. *Dah* walked in as he did every morning with heavy clomps made by his work boots, sat down at the table with eyes only half open, and drank his coffee in his usual ten minutes. Then he rolled his bacon strips in a slice of bread and was out the door without a word.

Sometimes he would give a dinner or supper order if he had a craving for something specific. He might say, "I expect a mess of fried chicken on the table when I get back," or "Don't forget the cornbread when you make the beans later," and then Elizabeth would have to scramble around to cook up a pot of dry beans without soaking them overnight first. If she couldn't get the food he wanted by the time he wanted it he would let out a groan and eat what was put in front of him, or pitch a fit and use it as an excuse to call her a *doomkupf*, or worse.

Then after supper he'd read the Bible with all his

daughters at the table and preach to them all like he were the bishop himself. He wanted them to believe it was because of God's word that he acted the way he did, calling it strict, rather than downright mean. Only she and her sisters knew how things really were. A nicer *Dah* could never be found than when they had company, which told Elizabeth he was quite aware of his sin, even if he'd never admit it.

Elizabeth scanned the pantry, making a mental note of what she would need to put on the grocery list for Thursday. For dinner she had planned a cheesy chicken noodle casserole. It wouldn't be too hard to make, and she knew Lydia would help.

"What's for breakfast?" Anna asked sleepily as she sat down at the table.

"What are you doing up so early? It's not time for you to get ready for school yet. Couldn't you sleep?"

She was still in her nightgown, her beautiful brown hair flowing down her back. Anna closed her eyes and tilted her head to the side, appearing to be asleep in the kitchen chair.

"You've got at least another hour. Go back to bed and I'll wake you when your breakfast is ready." She pushed Anna's shoulder, startling her.

"I can't. I have to be at school an hour early. We're taking a trip to the Schwartz's store today."

Elizabeth's mouth dropped open. "And when were you going to tell me this?"

"I'm sorry. I just forgot, I guess."

"Anna, you're twelve years old. When I was twelve I was taking care of everything around here and going to school as well. You can't even take care of yourself!"

"Don't yell at me, *schweshta*," she said lazily. "You know *Dah* doesn't like it when you yell at me." Anna's voice held

14

no remorse for her actions, but it wasn't a threat, only a simple observation. And she was right.

"*Dah's* already left the house. I can yell all I want."

"Well, I'm sorry I didn't tell you. Will you get me there early or do I need to walk?"

They both knew it was too far to walk. "Oh, all right. But try to be more courteous next time. I'm busy too, you know."

"Thank you, *schweshta*." She smiled. "Do you think maybe you could make me some pancakes for breakfast?" Her smile morphed into her pretty-please face.

Elizabeth huffed. If she thought those brown puppy-dog eyes would work on her she sure had another thing coming. "You'll be lucky if I give you a piece of burnt toast! Now go get your chores done and get ready for school." She shooed Anna out of the kitchen then shook her head.

Pancakes. The nerve of that girl. Asking for pancakes after the work she'd already caused, and she didn't even bat an eye to do it.

At least she was assertive. It was a quality Elizabeth admired in her youngest sibling. She wished she wouldn't have taken no for an answer with Nathan last night.

Maybe if I got Anna to ask for me. Elizabeth snickered to herself as she pulled the mixing bowl from the cabinet and got out the flour for the pancakes.

~

Thursday at noon, *Dah* came in early for dinner while Lydia was at Ada Hilty's quilting bee. Time always slowed down when she was in the house alone with *Dah*. Without her sisters present, his anger knew no limits.

Please help me God, not to cross him today.

Her hands moved quickly to put dinner on the table. When the food was in front of him she asked, "Can I get you anything else?"

"Just some peace and quiet while I eat," he grumbled, not looking up from his plate.

Her breathing was the only sound. Standing with one arm holding the other at the elbow she said, "Do you need anything from the market?" She asked only to remind him to give her some money for food before he left the house again.

"It's market day already? Don't we have plenty of food around here that needs eaten?" His dark brown eyes were boring a hole in his plate.

"Sure," she said carefully, her voice trained not to crack. "But we're all out of the soda you like so well."

Tense seconds passed.

Elizabeth's *vater* had acquired a taste for Mountain Dew and not the off-brand either. He popped the top on a can of the green bubbly stuff after dinner each day, taking it back with him to the fields or to the barn or even to town if that was what the day brought.

After the Amish open market, Elizabeth would need to stop at the local supermarket to pick it up. Lydia stayed home cooking, making sure supper was never late.

Elizabeth waited anxiously for his response, watching closely for his tells: clenching his teeth, jaws flexing slightly, or forcing his hand over his face in a sudden downward motion.

He groaned. The chair scraped the hardwood floor as he rose to his feet and pulled out his billfold. He handed her some money.

"One more should do it," she said as he started to close the billfold.

16

"I gave you extra last week, remember? I didn't have change, so I gave you an extra twenty."

"*Nay*, then you found change and gave me just enough, remember?"

"What are you tryin' to do? Make me think I'm losing my mind? I know what I gave you, and it was extra. Don't you still have it?"

Her heart sped. "I...don't, *Dah*. I don't have any extra." It was no use trying to explain to him that he really hadn't given it to her, but either way she didn't have it and she would need more money to buy the things they needed from the store.

"You've gone and spent it, haven't ya?"

She cringed, and her palms began to sweat. "*Nay, Dah.* I didn't."

"Don't you lie to me, girl. What have you been doing in town with my money?" He threw the billfold onto the table and grabbed her elbow, squeezing hard.

Her heart pounded in her ears. "I didn't do anything but buy groceries like you told me to."

"Liar!" He slapped her hard on her right cheek. She shut her eyes tight, waiting for the next blow.

"You ungrateful wench! I give you a place to live and food to eat, and this is how you repay me?"

Slap.

Her left cheek now matched the burning she felt in the other. She was his daughter and that was all he'd ever given her—that and a hard time.

Help me, God, to say the right things.

Elizabeth tried hard not to sob. "I'm sorry, *Dah*, please forgive me." She knew the only way out of his anger this time. "I bought Anna a new package of socks. I forgot. You were right," she lied.

17

He blew hot breath on her face from his nostrils, then he picked up his billfold and handed her another twenty. He returned the billfold to his back pocket and sat down at the table and began to eat as if nothing happened.

～

The open market was crawling with people. Some were *Englishers* but mostly Plain People, including Mennonites. On trips like these, Elizabeth pretended she was a free, independent woman with her own buggy and money to spend. Of course it wasn't true, and at this rate never would be, but it helped to get her mind off her real life, even if just for a few hours.

She picked up a jar of pickled okra at the table of a plump woman who had more wrinkles than a basset hound. She and Lydia both liked pickled okra but it wasn't on the list. Elizabeth set the jar back down.

Snatching up the jar, a man said, "If you don't want it, I'll buy it."

Looking up into Nathan Graber's face, Elizabeth's breath caught in her throat. It was unusual to see men without their wives or *mueters* strolling the open market, and a rare sight indeed to see them buying groceries.

"What are you doing here?" she asked.

"Just came after a few supplies," he said in a low voice and then handed the woman money.

The old woman behind the counter said, *"Danki,"* and Nathan smiled brightly. He turned with his jar of pickled okra and began to walk away.

"Wait," Elizabeth said and caught up with his pace. "Are you still leaving Monday?" She kept her voice low, trying not to let anyone overhear her, even though it wouldn't be a secret for long. He'd be the talk of Swan Creek Settlement in just a few days. And talk they would. Perhaps he was only keeping it a secret so people like Elizabeth wouldn't try to come along, or maybe so no one would try to talk him out of it.

"*Ja,*" he said. "I'd like to stay and chat, but I've got a lot of things to do before then. You understand, right?" He flashed another warm smile.

Elizabeth's breath caught. "*Ja.*" She shook her head. "I mean *nay.* Nathan, stop, please."

He stopped walking and turned to her with a loud breath. "What is it?" he asked, and raised his eyebrows expectantly.

Her heart began to race. This was her last chance to convince him to take her along. Her mind went blank.

What would Anna do?

"Please take me with you." She softened her eyes the way she imagined Anna would.

"I don't know, Elizabeth. This isn't your usual sight-seeing trip."

She thought quickly. "I'll get a job and help with the rent money. And I can cook and clean." She gasped at her own genius. "You aren't going to want to do your own laundry and make all your own meals, are you? Why, you can't eat out all the time, Nathan. That would simply cost too much money. Money you could spend on other things, right?"

"Well..." He shook his head slowly.

"I make the best cookies and cakes, oh, and pies. I can make any kind of pie you ever dreamed of." Her voice sped up with excitement. "And I'll fry up some chicken and make potato salad and I make the very best gravy you've ever had—everyone says so." She clasped her hands together tightly. "Oh, please, Nathan. I promise to keep the place spotless."

Elizabeth started to say more, but Nathan put up his hand. "You've convinced me. Be ready by eight." He shook his head at her with a smile as he turned to leave.

"You'll pick me up?" she asked quickly. His shaking head turned to a nod, but he didn't look back. Elizabeth stood there watching him disappear into the crowd, almost trembling with excitement. It wasn't until she remembered she had errands to run before supper that she realized she was biting her lip rather hard. She relaxed her jaw.

I'm going to Asheville.

She didn't want to let herself believe it. *Nay,* she shouldn't. Perhaps Nathan had just said it to get her to leave him alone. It would be a long weekend waiting to find out.

CHAPTER TWO

M onday morning, Elizabeth was up much earlier than usual, her stomach in knots and her breathing uneven. She paced the kitchen floor, waiting for time to pass so she could make everyone's breakfast.

What if he doesn't come?

Her heart sank at the thought, but that wasn't the worst thing that could happen. What if *Dah* saw what she was doing and stopped her? Would she ever get another chance?

This had to work.

Dah would eat his breakfast and leave the same as always, then she'd wake Lydia and give her instructions for the day's dinner and supper preparations. Then she'd wake Anna and take her to school early. But what if she didn't make it back in time? Elizabeth stopped and shook her head. *Nay,* Lydia would take her to school at the regular time. Then her sisters wouldn't be lying when they said they didn't see her leave.

She began pacing again. *Ja,* that would work. She wished she could say goodbye to Anna but it was too risky.

No one could know what she was doing. She would leave a note.

Elizabeth got a pen and paper and scratched one out, saying simply that she was leaving for *Rumspringa* with some of the youth and didn't know when she'd return. It was her right to go away for *Rumspringa* if she wanted. How else could one decide for sure if joining church was right for them? Oh, but why did it have to feel so sinful?

The clock finally said it was time to start *Dah's* breakfast. She got out the eggs she'd gathered yesterday and fumbled with the stove. Somehow she managed to get his food on the table despite the constant worrisome thoughts flooding her mind.

He entered and grunted as he scooted his chair in, the lines of his face showing his age.

"Do you need anything else?" she asked, wondering if it would be for the very last time. She doubted he'd ever let her back in the house after what she was going to do today.

He shook his head silently. It would be a little while before Anna would be getting ready for school. Usually she spent this time catching up on the mending or sweeping the floors, but today she was just too nervous. She pretended to dust the furniture in the living room until *Dah* finally walked out the back door.

An audible sigh escaped her lips. Elizabeth sat down at the table and put her feet up in the empty chair next to her, taking a whimsical look at her kitchen. It had belonged to her *mueter* before it became hers. She hadn't changed much about it in all these years, leaving the spoons and forks in the same drawer as always and the canisters in the same place on the counters. She'd often thought of how much more efficient it would have been to move things around but she never could bring herself to do it. Now it would be Lydia's kitchen.

She wouldn't miss it, yet she was satisfied with her accomplishments. Not everyone could run a house the way she had from the tender age of eleven. She tried to picture what her life would have been like if her *mueter* were still alive or if her *vater* had remarried like the bishop wanted him to.

Perhaps no woman would have him.

She often wondered what had made him so mean.

The back door opened and Elizabeth jumped up from her chair in surprise, almost knocking it over. *Dah* stood in the doorway.

Her heart raced. Why was he back so soon?

"The cows are out again." Then he turned around and disappeared into the yard.

Elizabeth's heart sank. Chasing cows back into the field wasn't a particularly hard job, but it often took hours. *Dah* had more cows than most anyone in the settlement. She hoped only a few had escaped, but it only took one unruly cow to ruin your whole morning.

Up the stairs she flew, and into Lydia's room. "Wake up, *schweshta*." Elizabeth shook her awake and watched her rub her eyes. "I've got to go help *Dah* with the cows. I need you to get breakfast and wake Anna and get her to school on time. There's a casserole in the fridge for you to heat up for supper tonight and some sandwiches already made for dinner."

"Why are you telling me all this?" she asked, her eyes still not fully opened.

"I'm going to Asheville. If I can get a ride, that is. Someone's supposed to pick me up at eight. I need you to take care of things while I'm gone. I'm counting on you to take care of Anna."

"Will you be back?" Her eyes were wide open now.

Elizabeth pressed her lips together. "Probably not. It's the group of youth I told you was going out on *Rumspringa*. You know how it is for me here. I hope to find a place of my own one day."

"In the community?" Her mouth gaped open.

"I don't know." She hated springing this on her all at once but what choice did she have? She'd hoped to at least sit down to breakfast with her one last time.

"You'll visit though, right?" Lydia was starting to get teary.

"I'll find a way to see you. I promise. Don't worry about me. I can take care of myself. But I have to go now. I've got cows to chase. I love you, *schweshta*. Tell Anna I love her, too."

Lydia nodded solemnly.

Elizabeth ran to her room and put on her shoes. She would need those in the *Englisher* world. Not many *Englishers* ran around barefoot all the time and some places in town wouldn't even allow you in without them. She grabbed her important papers and folded them up small, slipping them into the pocket of her dress. Next, she threw in her toothbrush and a small comb. Taking any extra clothes was out of the question. She'd never fit *them* in her dress pocket, deep as it was. *Dah* was waiting for her, probably red in the face already.

She lovingly touched the few items she had that belonged to her *mueter*, including the quilt on her bed, hoping that Lydia and Anna would take care of them for her. She placed the note on her pillow and ran from the room.

Outside, Elizabeth's fears had been realized. Huge, black cows dotted the yard. Had they been milk cows she could have led them to the barn easily with a bucket of grain at milking time, but these were beef cattle.

"Where you been?" *Dah* yelled as she approached.

"I had to wake Lydia," she said matter-of-fact, hoping he'd leave it at that.

"Get over by the garden and scare them this way. I'll hold the gate." He unlatched the gate beside him, ready to open it when the cows came through but not willing for any others to make their way out.

She hurried to the garden, careful not to scare them further away from the intended destination. Cows were big and could hurt someone badly if they stepped on a person, but for the most part, they were just big fraidy cats who moved fairly easily when you spooked them right, usually by running at them with arms stretched out wide. Giving a loud holler helped as well.

Elizabeth ran around them when they tried to go any direction but the gate. Slowly, she drove five of them right to *Dah*. He shut them in quickly and Elizabeth rounded up another set. Sometimes when a few cows went one way the others would follow suit, making the job easier. Only a few had the courage to go against the herd and try to do their own thing. Much like their people.

Elizabeth glanced at the road. She doubted they would be finished by eight. Was there any way she could leave with her *vater* watching? And how would she explain Nathan's visit?

She heard a holler from behind her. "I can help a while," Lydia said, "till it's time for Anna to go to school."

Elizabeth smiled at her sister and together they rounded up several more cows. It was a much easier task with more people. Soon Anna had finished her breakfast and was helping too. When school time came there was only one ornery cow left.

"You take Anna on to school, Lydia, and I'll finish up here," she said so *Dah* could hear. Lydia gave her a knowing look and obediently went to the horse stalls to hitch up the buggy.

At least she didn't have to make up an excuse for breaking their usual routine. Elizabeth had always done all the errands away from the house but Lydia could handle a horse and buggy just as well, and it was good that she was going to get the practice.

She watched the open buggy disappear with her sisters, hoping she'd see them again soon. It hadn't occurred to her until right then that Anna would probably be angry with her. After the initial shock and hurt had worn down she was angry with *Mah*. Elizabeth had been like a *mueter* to her ever since *Mah* died.

Pushing the painful thought to the furthest corner of her mind, Elizabeth ran after the cow. *Dah* would be busy fixing fence as soon as this task was complete, so preoccupied with his chores he wouldn't even notice anyone coming up the lane.

Good thing he didn't discover the cows were out before he ate his breakfast.

Elizabeth's stomach growled. Lydia had surely left her something to eat on the table. The only thing standing in the way of her freedom was one lone cow and she wasn't about to let it stop her from leaving.

Not today.

The cow veered left and Elizabeth ran left shooing it back. It ran right, heading for the driveway. Once it started down the lane it would keep on going, possibly taking the rest of the day to get back. She couldn't let that happen.

She swung around wide, running as hard as she could to head off the cow. It stopped and let out an angry breath.

"Back up!" Elizabeth yelled, hoping by now it knew what the command meant. It dipped its head quickly then took off past her, thundering down the lane.

"Not today!" she whined, stomping her foot hard on the ground. "You're going the wrong way, *doomkupf!*" She ran after it, trying her best to keep up but it was moving too fast. The driveway was a one-lane, quarter-mile long dirt path with a straggling line of grass down the middle, and fencing on both sides. The only way to get the cow back now would be to hope it stopped to graze in the ditch before hitting the main road. Then she could slip past and drive it back toward home.

She watched the cow disappear around the corner, still at full speed.

This can't be happening. Of all the days for the cows to get out, did it have to be this one?

Elizabeth held her aching sides. Out of breath, she walked at a steady pace and made her way to the corner, gravel crunching beneath her feet. A crow cawed in the distance. *Dah* would be heading this way as soon as he grew tired of waiting by the gate.

She wondered what time it was. If she left the driveway she might miss Nathan when he came by. *Nay*, if the cow went that far she'd have to head back home and get the horse.

Honk!

The long, loud sound of a car horn. The corner in the road dipped down low, hiding the other side. Elizabeth ran hard. A red car came into view, the cow in front of it. It stomped by Elizabeth, narrowly missing her, heading toward the house.

"I hope that's the way you wanted it to go," Nathan yelled from the open window.

"It sure is!" She hadn't expected him to arrive in a car. She guessed she should have. "You're early."

"We were all a little excited to get going. Get in." He nodded his head in the direction of the backseat.

James sat up front with Nathan. Elizabeth opened the back car door. There sat Rebecca Christener wearing a tee shirt and denim pants, her long brown hair hanging loose over her shoulders. On the other side of her, James's brother, Pete. At least the men were still wearing their plain clothes.

"*Vie gatz.*" She huffed as she got in and shut the door. Her breathing was still hard from running, her back damp from sweat. She rubbed her hands on her dress.

"Hey, Elizabeth," James said from the front seat, his sweet smile an apparent attempt at flirting. The car began to move up the driveway.

Her heart stopped. What would she tell *Dah?*

"Are there more cows out?" Nathan asked.

"*Nay,* this is the last one." Her mind raced through her options. "*Dah* can get it. I know you're ready to leave now. You can just turn around wherever you can find a spot." But she knew as soon as the words left her mouth there wasn't anywhere to turn around except her yard.

"*Nay,* we'll help you get the cow in."

Up the drive they went, the cow running ahead of them. When they reached the yard, the cow ran right for the gate on the other side of the property where *Dah* stood.

Thank you! she prayed. "Look there—right in. Thanks so much for your help, Nathan. We can go now. Just turn around right here." Elizabeth's heart threatened to break free from her chest.

"Don't you want to get your things?" he asked.

"Oh, I've got everything I need right here." Elizabeth pulled her toothbrush and comb from her pocket and showed it to him before quickly shoving it back in. "See. I'm ready as ever."

"*Guete*. We're going to get some new clothes today, too. But don't you want to say goodbye to your *dat?*" His eyebrows scrunched together in the reflection of the little mirror up front.

"*Nay!* I mean...we already did that and it's just...too painful to go through again."

"All right," he said, nodding his head in understanding. He began turning the car around.

Maybe *Dah* wouldn't even see her in the car. He'd know everything when Lydia returned and pretended to wonder about where she had gone. Then she'd find the note Elizabeth had left on the bed and act as surprised as he was about it.

She wiped her sweaty palms on her dress and watched as *Dah* fastened the gate, the cows now all safely inside.

"Are you all right?" Pete asked.

"*Ja*," she said quickly. "I'm sorry. I didn't even ask how you were today."

"*Guete*," he said, still eyeing her suspiciously.

Silence followed.

She chanced one more look behind them before the house disappeared. *Dah* stood in the yard where the car had turned around, scratching his head.

29

CHAPTER THREE

"**I**s everyone ready to see the apartment?" Nathan asked as he turned down a side street past the drugstore in Asheville. Elizabeth's stomach lurched at each curve. Maybe it was a *guete* thing she'd missed breakfast.

The image of her *vater* standing in the yard was still etched in her mind. She couldn't believe she was brave enough to defy him that way. What had gotten into her? This wasn't how proper ladies behaved. Then she remembered how improperly her *vater* behaved. She had to leave. Living with *Dah* was no kind of life at all.

"You mean you already rented one?" Rebecca asked.

"I sure did. Well, James, Pete and I did. We made arrangements last Thursday. Don't worry, you two ladies can pitch in however and whenever you're able."

"Any idea where we can find work?" Rebecca asked.

Elizabeth's eyes opened wide. She wasn't a proper young lady anymore. She was an *Englisher* woman who had to get a job. She took a deep breath and swallowed hard. Who would want to hire her? And would Nathan send her home if she couldn't find work?

"We'll buy a newspaper when we stop to get gas...after we have dinner." Nathan pulled into a driveway of a house much smaller than any of them were used to.

"Wait—lunch," James said with a laugh. "We're *Englisher* now, remember? We gotta' start talkin' like it."

No one laughed at his attempt at a joke. They were all too busy staring at the house. It didn't look run-down exactly, but it certainly lacked the homey appeal of houses in the community with flower beds and wheelbarrows and other evidence that someone cared for the place. It had a wooden privacy fence surrounding the yard and the exterior was made of rust-colored brick, giving a hard, unfriendly look to it.

"Well, what do you think?" Nathan asked.

Rebecca craned her neck over Pete. "Looks *guete* from out here. Let's see the inside."

"Oh, it's nice in there, too." Pete stretched his legs.

"You've seen it?" Elizabeth asked as they all got out.

"Thursday. Bedrooms are already set so don't get any ideas." Pete got a small bag from the trunk as did the others. Nathan slammed the trunk shut and they filed up the walkway to the door.

Nathan put the key in and said, "We'll have more keys made later today, so everyone can come and go as they please. The doors have to stay locked here at night. Don't anybody forget." It was common for people in the community to leave their doors unlocked any time of day or night, and some didn't even bother to lock up when they left for church or town. She clutched her comb through her dress pocket and peered over his shoulder.

Inside was a small living room with a couch that resembled the one at the doctor's office, a plush tan carpet, and bright red curtains that in some strange way matched. The kitchen sat beyond it with a stove built right into the cabinet space, and a nook beyond that held appliances Elizabeth had never seen before.

"The first bedroom is ours," Nathan said, pointing down the hall. "Then there's an indoor toilet and on the other side will be the ladies' bedroom."

Elizabeth glanced at Rebecca, hoping she could learn to enjoy her company.

Nathan clapped his hands together, still addressing the group, "All right. Let's get settled in. We have a few hours before" —he thought a second— "lunch." He smiled, obviously pleased with his *Englisher* speech.

Elizabeth followed Rebecca to their new room. It was tiny and there was only one bed, big enough for one person. Rebecca put her hands on her hips and huffed.

Elizabeth stopped beside her. "You take the bed. I can sleep on the floor. It's no problem," she said with a smile. There was a small night stand but no other furniture—not that any more would fit.

"Perhaps we should move the bed to the wall, to make more room?" Elizabeth asked. Rebecca nodded and they pushed and pulled till the bed was against the wall rather than in the middle of the room, freeing up an area for Elizabeth to lie down without fear of being stepped on during the night.

"Well, now what do we do?" Rebecca asked. It was the first time Rebecca had spoken to her the whole trip.

"I don't know," Elizabeth said. "What's this door to? A closet?" She opened it, peeking inside. "It's an indoor toilet."

"Let me see." Rebecca came over to investigate. She stood at the mirror, looking at herself when a door on the other side of the bathroom opened.

James stood looking at them. "Hey, Rebecca. You found the toilet, too?" His toothy grin made Elizabeth chuckle.

"These doors better have locks," Rebecca said, examining one of them.

"They do, but you'll have to lock both of them if you want any privacy," he said.

"*Ja*, I realize that now, *danki*."

"Well, I'll see you around, housemate," he said and shut the door in her face. Elizabeth turned around to keep Rebecca from seeing her smile. Living with this group was going to be very interesting.

~

A ll five of the "housemates," as James called them, stood in line at the Asheville McDonald's where the smell of grease was thick in the air. The menu looked like a television screen and kept changing as Elizabeth tried to read it. She rubbed her eyes and tried again. Workers behind the counter were flitting around like birds, hopping to and fro trying to get everyone's order. She watched Rebecca ask for a salad and pay for it with a twenty dollar bill.

Elizabeth discreetly moved to the other side of their group to speak with Nathan privately. "I don't have any money. I'm sorry. I should have asked *Dah* for some. I'm such a *doomkupf* sometimes." Her stomach growled.

"No worries, little lady." He put his arm around her shoulder. It was much more forward than any of the young men would do back home, but they weren't home anymore. They were in a whole new world with new rules altogether. "We'll all have jobs soon enough. I'll pay for your dinner and you can fix us supper, how does that sound?"

She let out a breath. "I'd be glad to. Did you get any groceries?"

"A few things. To tell the truth, I really didn't know what to buy." His voice was a whisper now. "Would you want to go shopping with me later?"

"I'd like that very much."

He smiled and she gazed at his soft, hazel eyes glittering in the hard lights.

"May I take your order?" the plump woman behind the counter asked.

"Order whatever you want," Nathan said to Elizabeth.

"I've never eaten here before." She looked up at the screen again, blinking rapidly. "There are just so many choices. There must be twenty different sandwiches."

"Here's what I do. Pick a number between one and" — he scanned the menu, pointing at it as he did—"seven."

"Okay...two," she said, wondering what that had to do with sandwiches and fried potatoes.

"She'll have a number two and I'll have a number one, please."

"Okay," the lady said, pushing some buttons. Nathan handed her the money and she gave him his change with a ticket, a large number written across the top. "You're number five forty-six. Who's next?"

Nathan motioned with a quick tilt of his head for her to move over to the side. Another worker quickly slammed two Styrofoam cups on the counter, each bigger than a quart jar, and pushed them their way.

Elizabeth's eyes widened. "That's a lot of water," she said.

"Well, you can get water or any other drink. They have tea and all kinds of soda. You just have to get it yourself, over there." He pointed to the drink machine.

"Do you have a trick for picking those?" she asked playfully.

"I usually just get tea," he said with a childish grin.

The knots in Elizabeth's stomach were finally starting to loosen. They filled their drink cups and waited for their number to be called. When it was, Nathan took their tray of food and they sat down at a big table with the rest of the group.

There were no knives or forks or even plates, and the weight of the massive tea cup worried Elizabeth with every sip, that it might break if she squeezed it too tight, but her hunger was extreme and she soon finished her number two, fried potatoes and a huge sandwich that looked no different from Nathan's number one.

"Are all the places to eat like this one?" Elizabeth asked.

"You mean with burgers and fries?" Nathan shoved a stack of fried potatoes in his mouth.

"*Nay,* I mean all the paper and no silverware." She licked the salt from her fingertips as she sat back in her seat, finally satisfied.

"Oh, then *ja,* they're all the same," Nathan answered and continued with his number one.

"*Nay,*" said Rebecca. "Some have silverware. Didn't you ever eat in town with your *Dat?*" She waved her plastic fork as she spoke.

"*Nay.* I remember going to a *café* once. Before *Mah* died. I don't remember where it was, though."

Rebecca looked down at her salad and a silence fell over the table. Elizabeth shifted in her seat.

"So what kinds of jobs do you think there will be for us?" Rebecca asked after some time passed.

"Mmm." Nathan chewed his food a few seconds before answering. "There's a gas station across the street. I'll go get

35

a paper and we'll all look together." He stood and wiped his hands on his trousers.

"Finish your food, Nathan." Rebecca motioned for him to sit. "It can wait."

"*Nay,* it's okay. I'm excited, too. Maybe we can go talk to someone when we leave here. I'd like to have a job by the end of the day."

"For sure," Pete said, nodding his head in agreement, his mouth full.

James grabbed Nathan's arm as he walked by. "Can you get me a girlfriend by the end of the day?" James batted his eyes as he looked up at him.

Nathan shook his head and James burst into a fit of laughter.

~

The stove was electric. Elizabeth turned the knob at the top and watched a red swirl magically appear beneath the black glass top. Her hand hovered over it. Almost instant heat. She set the skillet down light as a feather, not wanting to scratch the pretty stovetop. The cookware Nathan had purchased was from the dollar store and not made with quality materials like the heavy ones at home. She hoped it would cook the same. She was counting on her cooking skills to impress Nathan—and to pay him back for bringing her to Asheville and buying her dinner and a couple sets of new clothes.

It had been difficult shopping. She'd never worn anything that wasn't homemade before except socks and shoes, and she only wore those during the coldest months. She settled on one long-sleeve tee-shirt and one short. Then Rebecca had helped her find skirts to match them both.

They were long and flowing, and the soft material had a flower pattern. Back home they weren't even allowed to have flower patterns on the dishes, much less their bodies. Wouldn't Lydia be surprised.

She sighed.

Thoughts of Anna pierced her heart. Elizabeth wondered how angry she was about her leaving, but it was for the best. Everyone would get along much better without her.

Elizabeth heated the shortening in the skillet and rolled the meat in flour. Soon she would find a way to speak with Lydia. Perhaps on market day. For now she would concentrate on being a productive and helpful member of the group. Without them she would have to return home and that wasn't an option.

Rebecca had gone to see if there were any places to work within walking distance, and the guys went to inquire about an ad they saw in the paper for a new sawmill on the edge of town. By the time the men arrived back, supper was ready.

Elizabeth set plates and silverware they had purchased in the camping section of Wal-Mart on the table. Then, not seeing any extra dishes to use for serving, she took each plate up and filled it with the food before setting it back in its place. Each plate held fried pork chops, mashed potatoes and white gravy, and corn on the cob. She would have made more food if she'd had more dishes to work with.

"Mmmm, somethin' smells *guete*," James said before he entered the kitchen. Elizabeth smiled.

"Where's Rebecca?" Nathan asked from behind him.

"She went down the street to see if there were any places for us to work. She should be back any time, but no need in letting the food get cold. You three sit down and eat." Elizabeth stood out of the way, allowing them more room to enter the small kitchen. They sat down and Elizabeth brought them each a soda from the fridge. "I doubt it's very cold yet," she said.

"It's just fine, Elizabeth. Sit with us." Nathan watched her until she finally sat down in the chair beside him. "Well, now I guess we pray," he said. They all bowed their heads for a moment of silence until Nathan cleared his throat to indicate they were finished. He took a bite of his pork chop. "Mmmm. This is *sehr gut*, Elizabeth." He smacked his lips. "I'm sure glad I talked you into coming." He smiled playfully.

Elizabeth just shook her head, but inside her heart the comment danced. "Did any of you get a job?"

Nathan wiped his mouth with his fingertips. "We did. Well, we had to tell them we'd throw James in for free, but they finally agreed."

James had a mouthful of corn on the cob and couldn't defend himself. Pete set his fork down. "He said to be there by six. Does anyone have an alarm clock?" he asked.

"Nope," James said and began gnawing away at his corn again.

Pete furled his eyebrows. "What do we do? Just take turns sleeping? He seemed like a pretty strict guy. I don't think he'll let us work if we're a minute late."

Elizabeth spoke up. "I'm always up between four and five. I'll wake you."

"Why do you get up that early?" Nathan asked.

"*Dah* likes an early breakfast."

"What about your sisters?" Pete asked.

"I wake them after he leaves the house and we all eat breakfast together before I get Anna off to school." She picked at the mashed potatoes on her plate with her fork.

38

"So," Pete rocked the corn cob back and forth with his wrist as he spoke, "you're kind of like the *mueter* of the house, huh?"

"Since I was eleven."

"I bet that was rough," Nathan said.

Elizabeth just nodded.

"Well, I'll bet your *vater* misses you something awful then." Nathan opened his soda with a spewing sound.

Elizabeth pressed her lips together, not sure what to say.

"He's missing out on a mighty good pork chop with you being away. I can say that for sure." He smiled and took another big bite.

"Guess what?" Rebecca called from the living room. She strutted in wearing the new clothes she bought, a tight pair of denim shorts, which it would soon be way too cool for, and a tank top that left all the guys in the house slurring their words when she was around. "I got a job!" Her smile went from ear to ear.

"Doing what?" Elizabeth asked.

"There's an old lady down the street that needs some help with yardwork. She's got all the equipment, lawn mowers and things. She said if I do a *guete* job she'd let me clean out her garage and then the tool shed. Her husband died a few years ago and she said she wants to get all his junk out of there before she dies."

"Rebecca," Elizabeth admonished.

"What? That was exactly how she said it. *Englishers* are strange. Anyway, what's for supper?" She eyed the table.

"I can make you a plate." Elizabeth jumped up and quickly filled another dish for Rebecca. She couldn't understand a person getting rid of all their loved one's possessions when they died. *Englishers* were strange.

"The guys got jobs, too," Elizabeth said as she handed her the plate.

"Nice. Well, I guess you're the only one left, then."

Elizabeth's breath caught. Just what would an *Englisher* want her to do?

"Elizabeth," Nathan asked, matter of factly, "can you make apple dumplin's?"

"Of course," she said.

"And what about raisin pie?" Pete asked, his hair black as a crow's feather.

"You mean the kind they make for weddings? *Ja.*"

"And can you make rhubarb cobbler?" James asked, finally done with his corn on the cob.

"*Ja.* Who couldn't? Wait—are you suggesting I bake for *Englishers?*" Her face scrunched up tight.

"Actually, I was thinking about you cooking for *us.* Three meals a day?" Nathan raised his eyebrows.

"And desserts," Pete added.

"And desserts," Nathan repeated.

"And rhubarb cobbler," James said, trying to follow suit.

"Well, of course I will, fellas. If I had the right pans and ingredients I'd make them all right now, but I still need a job to make money."

Nathan shook his head. "*Nay,* you won't. You either, Rebecca. We found jobs that will support us all. You ladies can stay here and keep house while we work."

Rebecca huffed. "Elizabeth can stay here if she wants, but I'm tired of cooking and cleaning. I've done it every day since I can remember. I'm getting a job or I'm out." She lifted a hand loosely in a wide-eyed, palm-up gesture then began eating again.

"Then it all falls on you, Elizabeth. Can you feed us all?" Nathan asked.

Elizabeth blinked back her joy. "Of course I can. And I'll keep the house clean and even do the laundry. And whatever else needs done around here."

"Then it's settled. Tomorrow we begin our new life as *Englishers*." Nathan slapped the table to conclude the meeting then left the room, the others following after him, Rebecca taking her plate with her, leaving Elizabeth alone in silent awe of her new kitchen.

～

E lizabeth opened her eyes to the sound of a toilet flushing in the next room. She had slept in her old clothes, not willing for anyone to see the ragged slip she used as a nightgown. She twisted up her hair quickly and tied her *kapp* on. There was no reason for shoes until the next trip to the store, so she left them in the corner near where she'd slept on the floor. Nathan had given her an extra blanket, the thick kind found in their open buggies during winter. The air in the house was warm enough she'd used it for a pillow. The plush carpet felt strangely comfortable between her toes as she made her way to the kitchen.

She rubbed her eyes and followed the only light in the house—in the kitchen. She found Nathan fumbling with a coffee pot on the countertop.

"I thought I was supposed to wake you and here you are waking me," she said.

He turned, meeting her eyes. "I'm sorry. I didn't mean to. I'm just excited to see if this job is going to work out for all of us."

"Well, can I help you with that?"

"*Ja*. Do you know how to work it?"

She looked at the strange contraption with all its

41

buttons. She pushed one of them and the red light blinked and numbers appeared on the tiny screen. She pushed it again and another number came up.

"I'll tell you what. I'll make some coffee on the stove and you can decide if you want to figure it out. Deal?"

He laughed. "Sometimes the old ways are the best, aren't they?"

"In this case I'd say for sure." Elizabeth got out a shiny new pan she'd put in the cabinet the night before. It was strange but exciting working in a new kitchen.

Nathan sat down at the table. "I see you're still dressing plain today."

Elizabeth set down the plastic coffee can she'd just picked up. "Oh, I'm sorry, Nathan. I forgot. I really do appreciate the clothes you bought for me. I'll go put them on right now." She started to leave the kitchen.

"Wait. I don't care what you dress like, but the others..." He thumbed in the direction of the back hall bedrooms. "They're here for the full *Englisher* experience, you know? Maybe after breakfast?"

"*Ja.* I understand." She turned back to the stove.

"So, why are you here?"

She stopped, glad she wasn't facing him. "Well...you know, to experience the outside world before joinin' church."

"So you're sure you'll join?" he asked in a friendlier-than-usual voice.

"*Nay.*" She hadn't really thought about it until right then. Maybe because she never realized she had a choice. "You?"

"I don't know, either. I thought I did. But I think the next few weeks will tell me."

42

Elizabeth poured a cup of coffee in a blue tin cup and set it in front of him. "Eggs and bacon okay for breakfast?"

"*Ja. Danki.* I mean thank you."

She laughed.

"What?" he said.

"You can take the man out of the settlement but you can't take the settlement out of the man."

"We'll see about that." Nathan took a sip of his coffee. "*Sehr gut,* Elizabeth. I mean... Oh, you know what I mean." He smiled.

"Let the coffee work, Nathan. Then you can work on becoming an *Englisher.*" She laughed. "I'll get you some breakfast. That's sure to help as well."

In no time at all she had breakfast on the table and excused herself to change. It felt very strange taking her *kapp* off during the day. She unpinned her hair but then pinned it back up again, not sure how she would even do dishes with it down and in her way. The new clothes were soft but still felt odd. Seeing the splashes of so many colors from the corner of her eye was distracting as she walked back into the kitchen.

"That's really pretty," Nathan said.

She stopped, meeting his eyes. "*Danki.*"

He stared at her a moment and said, "Well, I'd better get the fellas up."

Elizabeth nodded to him and went about setting plates for everyone. She wondered at the way Nathan had chosen the word pretty then shook it off. It wasn't *guete* to fill her head full of those kind of thoughts. She supposed Nathan would have himself an *Englisher* girl before the week was out.

43

CHAPTER FOUR

lizabeth's eyes narrowed. "I thought barbeque was a sauce you put on grilled meat." She stood in the living room with arms crossed, waiting for Nathan to explain.

It was Saturday evening and Nathan had invited one of the men he worked with over for supper. "It's a cookout, but it's more than just that with the *Englishers*."

"So *you're* going to do the cooking?" Elizabeth asked inquisitively. "I thought..."

"Carlos said the men are supposed to stand outside and drink beer while they cook the meat and potatoes on the grill."

"Carlos, huh?" she muttered, still trying to wrap her head around why men would want to cook on their day off.

"He said he was going to teach us how to be *Englishers*."

"Ah. Well, what do the women do during these frolics?"

"I'm not sure. I can ask." He slipped his boots on as a truck pulled into the driveway. "I know. Why don't you make up some desserts? I'll bet Carlos never had anything like you can make."

44

Elizabeth liked the sound of that. "I'll get right on it. Let me know if I'm supposed to do anything else."

Nathan slipped out the door and Elizabeth watched him greet his friend from the living room window.

An *Englisher* in the house. Well, at least it was only one extra person for supper. She'd probably have to cook for everyone after they burned all the good meat, but she'd manage somehow.

~

Several lawn chairs dotted the small fenced-in backyard of the rental house. James stepped up to the sliding glass door and called through the screen to Rebecca and Elizabeth inside. "Food's ready, ladies." He peeked in, his hand blocking the sun from his eyes.

"You ready for this?" Rebecca asked Elizabeth.

Of course she wasn't. Everyone was about to see her parade around with her hair down and paint on her face like some floozy *Englisher* woman. Rebecca had insisted.

Is making friends worth this?

At least she was fully covered in her skirt and long sleeve shirt. She'd been wearing her old dress while she cooked and cleaned, especially if no one else was around, and new clothes when they went out, but this evening they had company, making it a special occasion.

Rebecca had on her tight shorts and a low-cut blouse with a thin jacket over it. It was all Elizabeth could do to keep from zipping it up to hide some of her skin. She'd even gone as far as braiding her hair.

Rebecca nudged her out the door where the four men stood, each with a can of beer in their hand. The sight took Elizabeth back to a time after *Mah* died when *Dah* began

45

buying cases of the stuff. After many weeks, he woke up one morning with his face inches from the pond and swore he'd never touch the stuff again. That was when the Mountain Dew habit started. Until then, Elizabeth believed it was the beer that had made him mean.

She should have expected it. Of course the guys would want to experiment with alcohol while on *Rumspringa*, but how far would they take it?

The smoke from the grill stung her eyes. Her stomach growled. Carlos stopped talking as she and Rebecca approached, his eyes wide. "Well, hello, ladies. Fellas, you didn't tell me you'd invited beautiful women to this shindig. I'm Carlos," he said, holding out his hand to each of them.

After shaking hands, Elizabeth sat down in a lawn chair while Rebecca made her move. Rebecca's eyes followed him with the attention of a barn cat when a mouse is near.

"I'm Rebecca Christener. It's so good to meet you." She smiled, her perfect brown hair braided to the left side. She looked just like an *Englisher* girl now but Elizabeth figured she must, too. It felt weird, wearing a costume all the time and painting your face, but it was harder to be the only one in the house who dressed plain.

"It's good to meet you, too, both of you." He eyed Elizabeth. A handsome man, Carlos was trim and well-built, with jet-black hair and dark eyes. His skin was a few shades darker than most and it gave him a completely exotic appearance. Elizabeth wondered where he was from. *Certainly not Asheville, Missouri.*

"Are these brutes here your brothers?" he asked. He had no noticeable accent. Perhaps it was his parents who were from afar.

"*Nay,*" Rebecca said. "I mean, no. We're just friends." She stood close by his side and lightly touched his arm.

"Well..." Nathan said. "The food's ready. Everyone get a plate. And when we're done I believe Elizabeth has some dessert made inside. Is that right?"

"*Ja.* I made the apple dumplin's you've been asking about. And there's ice cream to go with them in the freezer." Elizabeth debated whether or not to cross her legs in the chair that sunk low to the ground.

Nathan clapped his hands together and turned to Carlos. "That sounds fantastic. You're in for a treat, Carlos. Elizabeth's a wonderful cook."

"Oh, really?" Carlos raised his eyebrows.

James piped up, "You won't catch us complaining."

Nathan made a plate of food and handed it to Elizabeth. "She feeds us well."

She touched her fingers to the base of her throat. "Oh, Nathan." She shook her head. "I can get my own plate. You go ahead and eat."

"*Nay,* you deserve a rest. That's what the whole barbeque thing is about. I think."

"I thought it was about beer," James said, grabbing another one from a large blue cooler full of ice.

Elizabeth searched his face. No man had ever brought her food before. *"Danki."*

It looked good. She took it with both hands, savoring the smell of perfectly cooked meat. So she'd been wrong about their ability to cook, but was he just being nice—or something more?

"Donkey?" Carlos said inquisitively.

"Danki, it means thank you," Elizabeth corrected.

"Ah, in your Amish language. So is that like Pennsylvania Dutch?" Carlos sat down in the chair next to her as Nathan began assembling another plate of food.

"*Nay.* We speak a Swiss German dialect. It's very different. In fact, if we met someone from Pennsylvania we'd need to speak English to understand one another."

"Fascinating."

Elizabeth eyed the can of beer as it went to his lips and then back down to his lap. She supposed it was customary for *Englishers* to drink socially, but her eyes still strayed to the can more often than not.

"Have you ever met any Pennsylvania Amish?" Carlos asked.

"*Nay,* but my cousins have. They say the first thing they want is to hear us yodel." She smiled and then wondered why Carlos was so fascinated with their Amish ways. She looked over to see Rebecca sitting down in another chair on the other side of the grill with Pete and James. Nathan stood hovering over the grill, a loud sizzle as he turned the last few burgers.

"You yodel?" he asked with raised eyebrows, his voice becoming higher pitched at the end.

"*Ja,* but they don't. I believe it's the High German they speak. Somehow it won't let their voice free."

"Are there other differences?" He leaned toward her in his chair, a wide grin growing across his face.

"Of course. We don't even share the same ancestors so there are many."

"Well," Carlos said, "I can already tell that your kind is more interesting." He gave her a look like a fox eyeballing a chicken.

A tingle coursed down her spine.

"Um....I'd better go get a drink." Elizabeth started to get up when Nathan stopped her.

"You sit down and I'll get you something. What would you like?" he asked.

Elizabeth shifted in her chair, certain she'd never had a

man wait on her before and wondering what it all meant. "Maybe a soda?" she said finally. Back home she wasn't even allowed to drink *Dah's* soda, but she had it occasionally at church dinners or frolics.

"I'll get you one from the fridge. Be right back. What about you, Rebecca?" He turned to face her but she already had a beer in her hand and was shaking her head.

Elizabeth's scalp prickled. Was it from not wearing her *kapp* or because Nathan was leaving her there with Carlos, who seemed much more interested in her than she was comfortable with. She cleared her throat, shifting away from him in her chair.

"Tell me, Liz," he lowered his voice almost to a whisper, "are all the Amish girls as pretty as you are under those *kapps*?"

No one had called her Liz before and it wasn't right to talk in public about how pretty people were.

Is there nothing an Englisher won't say?

She felt her cheeks getting warm. "Um...well, my sisters are both much prettier than I'll ever be. They have chocolate-brown hair and brown eyes like my *Dah*." It hadn't occurred to her in a long while that she was the only one with blue eyes and blonde hair, just one more way she felt like the odd duck of the family.

"You're quite likely the most beautiful woman in Asheville. If they don't look like you I bet they wish they did."

Elizabeth cleared her throat again and then took a big bite of her burger. Nathan handed her a bottle of soda over her shoulder.

"*Danki*," she said as soon as she could swallow.

"So," Nathan said loudly, "have we succeeded at our first attempt at a barbeque?"

49

"This is great, man," Carlos said. "The only thing that would make it better is more people."

James tossed Pete another beer. "And more girls," he said.

Nathan laughed. "Next weekend then? That ought to give us time to find more people, right?"

Carlos chuckled. "Oh, if you want people, I have lots of friends who'd love to eat this kind of food." Carlos got up and took a paper plate from the package and helped himself to a burger. Elizabeth's shoulders relaxed now that there was some distance between them, but talk of another get-together, one much bigger than this one, had her breathing shallow.

A house full of *Englishers?* More men like Carlos? Elizabeth's eyes traveled to each of her housemates. She let out a breath. Lydia and Anna wouldn't concern her half as much. She shook her head. Thoughts of her sisters always seemed to leave an achiness in her chest that was difficult to ignore.

Her housemates were nice enough, but did they know what they were getting themselves into? Leaving home and coming to Asheville was supposed to make her world bigger, so why did it suddenly feel so small?

The next morning, Elizabeth was awake much too early to start breakfast. She tiptoed past Rebecca into the bathroom. Slowly she shut the door and locked it, careful not to make more noise than necessary. The bright light reminded her of the restrooms in town, but she had to admit it was nice to sit on a toilet without traveling outside to get there. She spied the door to the men's bedroom.

Without any noise she turned the lock and let out a deep breath.

After doing her business, she washed her hands with hot water straight out of the tap and gazed into the mirror, wondering if the bishop was right. Did a mirror on a wall cause one to be vain any more than a small one stored in a drawer? She doubted seeing a larger reflection of herself a few times daily had changed her any. Perhaps with some people...

Her eyes were wide open. *No way to get back to sleep now.* She glanced at the shower curtain, bold red roses on a black background, and imagined the luxurious warm stream. Guilt washed over, but the cause escaped her. Didn't she deserve a hot shower whenever she wanted? She was an *Englisher* woman now, after all, and they were here to experience what the world had to offer. If she hurried, she'd still have time to be dressed and ready for the day before anyone else awoke.

Before she could change her mind, she took off her clothes and pulled back the shower curtain.

James!

She screamed and pulled the curtain around herself. He was lying fully dressed in the tub with beer cans around him. His arms flailed, hitting the shower wall with hard thumps. He jumped up and screamed back at her.

"What is it?" he yelled, eyes darting around, his burly hands balled into fists that bounced up and down. He stumbled and fell out of the tub onto the floor at her feet.

Elizabeth screamed again.

He blinked his eyes and shook his head. The doors rattled.

"Elizabeth! What's going on in there?" one of the men called.

51

"Get out!" she yelled, holding the shower curtain tightly around her.

James looked up at her. "What'd you have to go and scare me like that for?" He shook his head as he stood to his feet, using the wall for support. One hand held his head. "You about gave me a heart attack!"

"Get out," she yelled again.

"I'm goin', I'm goin'," he said as he unlocked the door. Pete and Nathan pushed their way in as the door opened.

"Woah!" Nathan said when he caught sight of her. They stood in front of Elizabeth in nothing but long socks and shorts.

"Get out of here!" she screamed.

Nathan put his head down and they all headed back out of the room, but Rebecca was still beating on the other door. "What's going on?"

As soon as the mens' door was shut, Elizabeth ran to lock it. Then she threw her clothes back on with shaking hands and unlocked the door for Rebecca.

She peeked her head in. "What is all the screaming about?"

Elizabeth pushed her way out the door and stormed through the house all the way to the kitchen.

Pans rattled loudly as she pulled them aggressively from the cabinet and slammed them down on the countertop. She found the skillet she was looking for and set it down hard on the stovetop.

"You okay?"

She whirled around to find Nathan, fully dressed now, staring at her curiously.

A tense breath escaped her nose.

"James didn't hurt you, did he?" he asked.

She relaxed her tense forehead. Fire burned in her cheeks. *"Nay."*

"I didn't think so. He's harmless. A little dimwitted at times, but harmless."

"I'm just not used to this. I don't even have brothers."

"Well, maybe you're ready to go back home. I could take you."

"Nay!" she said quickly. "I'm fine. It just...startled me. I'm sorry I made such a fuss." If she wanted to stay she would have to learn to expect anything.

"I'll tell you what. It's supposed to be scorching hot today. Let's go swimming."

"What?" Men and women never swam together in the community.

"All of us. I know a good swimming hole that should still have some water. We can pack up some food and a cooler for the beer and spend the day."

"Do you think anyone will see us?"

"Nay, it's a church Sunday. No one will be about." He smiled, setting her mind at ease somewhat.

"All right," she said, but she still wasn't sure how it was going to work. She didn't even have clothes to swim in.

A few hours later the sun shone brightly on the bank of Swan Creek. The gravel crunched under their feet as they walked along to the spot Nathan directed. Elizabeth couldn't get past the shorts the men wore. At least they weren't shirtless like some of the *Englisher* men on hot days, but they had no sleeves and Elizabeth found herself staring at the roundness of Nathan's shoulder muscles.

"How far is it?" Elizabeth asked as they walked past a grove of sycamore trees, shade dotting the path in splotches on the dry rocks.

"You've never been to the bone hole?" Rebecca asked,

her tight tank top revealing all her curves—curves Elizabeth wondered if she even had.

Elizabeth shook her head. "What's the bone hole?"

Pete and James both had one end of a cooler and crunched along ahead of them.

Nathan walked a little closer to her. "It's not far. It's called the bone hole because there used to be a bone tied to the end of the rope."

"What rope?"

"The rope swing. Don't you ever go to the creek?"

"Sure," she said, "just closer to the house." Elizabeth tried to remember the last time she went swimming. It had to have been before *Mah* died. She wondered if she could still swim.

They arrived at the place James and Pete had set the cooler down. Elizabeth looked over the steep embankment made from light gray boulders to the creek below. A stick poked up precariously at the top of the path, marking their descent. They each took a can of beer or soda and leaving the cooler on the level ground, they carefully made their way down.

At the bottom, Elizabeth watched Nathan jump in without even testing the water first. It was early September and hot for this time of year, but the nights were starting to get cooler and Elizabeth had no idea what the water temperature would be like. She pulled at her tee-shirt, the walk to the creek leaving her sticky. Under her skirt was a skimpy pair of shorts Rebecca had loaned her.

Rebecca had on a pair even shorter and began walking into the water slowly. "That's cold!" Rebecca complained in a high-pitched voice.

Pete sat down on a huge rock in the shade and opened his beer while James approached. "I'm sorry about earlier,

Elizabeth," James said. "It was an accident, and it coulda happened to anybody." The apology in his eyes was heartfelt, but Elizabeth wondered if he realized that sleeping in a bathtub wasn't normal, *Englisher* or Amish. He held out his hand and she shook it.

"I forgive you." She had no choice, really. If she wanted to stay with the group in Asheville she needed to get along with everyone.

He smiled a toothy grin.

Nathan went under again and came up with water pouring off his chin. He let out a whoop that echoed in her ears.

"Come on, Elizabeth," Rebecca called.

"I thought you said it was cold."

"It is, but you get used to it."

Elizabeth looked down at her long skirt. It didn't feel right to take it off and show everyone her bare legs. She slipped off her only pair of shoes, not willing to risk ruining them. She contemplated leaving her skirt on. It was how the other girls in the community went swimming, and how they'd done it when she was young, but she hated to chance soiling the pretty skirt. She looked over at Nathan to find he was eyeing her.

"Come on, Elizabeth. The water's great!" he called.

She had to do it, she reasoned, to be a member of the group. She remembered the awkwardness of the shower incident that morning and how it had only served to further disconnect her from her housemates.

She slid off the skirt and ran into the water, not stopping until her legs were submerged. She drew in a deep breath, the cold water piercing her skin. Nathan laughed as she clenched her fists at her sides and gritted her teeth. Never had she gone without her dress in the light of day.

She peered into the water at her white legs. A small fish darted past, the sunlight making it look like a shiny piece of aluminum foil. Algae particles hovered above her knees. After a few minutes her legs grew strangely comfortable in the water and she ventured to walk a little deeper, careful not to fall on the slick rocks.

Nathan swam up to her, his wet head poking up from the water at waist level, eyes glittering in the sun. "Come on, Elizabeth, live a little," he said quietly, his voice alone enough to make her knees wobble.

"I'm in," she said. What more did he want?

"Do it all at once and in a few seconds you'll be glad you did."

He was suggesting she go completely under. She hadn't even considered getting her head wet. Her hair hung down, the ends in the water. She shook her head. "I can't. It's too cold."

"But you want to?" he asked.

"Well, I guess."

Nathan sprang from the water and hugged her tight, his bare arms touching hers, giving her a tingling sensation. She screamed as they fell sideways into the water, submerging her. He released her and she threw her head up and took a breath of air. Her heart beat erratically and the cold had her panting. Nathan smiled at her, now eye-level.

"What was that for?" She began to stand up, but seeing her shirt clinging to her chest she stayed low.

"You said you wanted in, I thought you looked like you could use some help."

Her mouth dropped open and she splashed him right in the face. He turned his head and laughed. Had all the rules of propriety gone out the window the second they left home? A few weeks ago she never would have dreamed she'd be in the creek half naked with Nathan Graber touching her. But he was right about jumping in. The water felt good already.

With dry hair, Rebecca walked to the bank and stretched out on a rock in the sunshine with a beer in her hand while Pete and James headed in. Gravel crunching under his feet, James ran for the water and splashed about, bending over to dunk his head. Pete walked in slowly behind.

"It's deeper over here," Nathan said, gesturing with a tilt of his head.

"Oh, I'm fine right here," Elizabeth said.

James made his way over to them. "Looks like the rope's still here."

Elizabeth looked up to the tree that bent over the water on the other side of the creek. A long rope with a stick tied to the end hung down just enough someone could reach it.

"Come on, Elizabeth, you can go first," Nathan said.

"That's quite all right," Elizabeth said. "You two go ahead." She watched a reckless grin pass between James and Nathan. James picked her up. She screamed as James hoisted her over his shoulder.

"Put her down," Pete called to him, but James began walking her toward Nathan.

"James! No!" she screamed as she watched the water come up further and further on James's waist. "Please!" He gave her a toss and she held her breath as she fell.

Her heart stopped. Suddenly her ears filled with water.

She opened her eyes. Frantically she felt for the bottom with her toes.

Where is it?

She stopped and seemed to hover there, her hair all around her.

Her arms flailed, her toes stretched out as far as possible trying to feel for the bottom.

Please, God, don't let me die like this.

How horrible to drown in Swan Creek, all because she was too ashamed to tell them no one had ever bothered to teach her how to swim.

She pushed her arms downward and kicked with her feet.

A hand squeezed her arm and then let go. Were they going to hold her under? Strong hands grabbed her waist and as she began to fight them the surface appeared. She took a deep breath, wiping the water and hair from her face with one hand, holding onto Nathan's arm around her with the other.

"Quit kicking," he said, "I got ya."

She turned and clung to him with a little cough. "Don't let me go." Her voice sounded more desperate than she realized it would. Her body trembled.

He brought her over to the place where she'd been standing when James had nabbed her. Still, she held onto him. He carried her to the bank and set her shaking body down on a big rock, hot from the sun.

Rebecca hovered over her. "Are you okay?" She slapped James's chest as he neared.

"What?" he said. "How was I supposed to know she couldn't swim?"

Pete gave him a stern look. "You don't do that to girls, you *doomkupf!*" He shook his head. "No wonder the community doesn't allow men and women to swim together."

Elizabeth's hands hadn't stopped shaking. She looked down at her bare legs. "Could someone hand me my clothes?"

Nathan was closest. He handed her the skirt and she covered herself with it like a blanket, the warmth soaking into her legs. "Are you all right, Elizabeth?"

Pete pushed James, even though his brother had a couple inches and at least twenty pounds on him, and Elizabeth wondered if it would end in a fight.

"I'm sorry," she said loud enough to get their attention. "It was my fault."

They all looked at her quizzically.

"I haven't been swimming since before *Mah* died. I should have told you I couldn't swim. I'm sorry and I hope I didn't ruin anyone's day."

"You've got nothing to be sorry about," Rebecca said.

"*Ja,*" they all agreed.

Elizabeth struggled to breathe amid their suffocating stares. She gasped.

Nathan cleared his throat. "Let's give her some space."

The group dispersed, leaving her alone with Rebecca. "James can be a *doomkupf* sometimes, but he means well."

Elizabeth smiled tightly. "You're the second person to tell me that today."

She smiled. "Well, it's true."

"It's okay, really. I'm fine."

Rebecca nodded slowly and then walked away. Elizabeth wished she hadn't wasted the opportunity to get closer to Rebecca, but perhaps later when she'd calmed down they could talk more.

Nathan came down the steep path and handed her a grape soda. It was ice cold in her hand with water beads running off it.

"*Danki,*" she said, still feeling strange about him waiting on her.

"I'm really sorry. I wouldn't have pulled you under if I

59

knew. And I certainly wouldn't have let James throw you in."

"It was my fault. I shouldn't have lied."

"Then why did you?"

"I guess I just wanted to fit in."

"With us?" He laughed. "You'd probably be better off just being yourself." He smiled. Perhaps he was right. Maybe she didn't have to lie to fit in, but it was certainly important enough to.

~

When Pete entered the kitchen that evening wearing his usual *Englisher* clothes, a snug tee-shirt and denim pants, Elizabeth stood. She was peeling potatoes at the table for Sunday supper.

"Can I help you with anything, Pete?" she asked. He was the quietest member of the group, and she doubted he would ever ask her for anything, but it was up to her to run the kitchen and feed everyone.

"No." He dug in the fridge and pulled out a wadded up piece of paper.

"What's that?" Had she seen it before she likely would have tossed it out.

"The rest of my burger from the other day." He'd saved it from when they'd gone to the drive-through days ago.

"I'll have supper ready in about an hour," she said. "I'm making a casserole with the leftover meat from the barbeque."

"Sounds *guete*. I'll just heat this up for a snack." He placed it in the little microwave on the counter.

"Do you really know how to use that thing?" she asked. She had to admit, she was curious about it. Ever since

Nathan had asked the landlord what it was she was dying to see how it worked, but she wasn't going to be the first one to touch it.

"*Nay*. But it can't be that hard." He started punching buttons but nothing happened.

"What about that one?" she asked, pointing to a button that said, "high."

He hit the button and it lit up with a hum. The glass dish in the bottom began to turn in a circle. They both stood close, hunkering down to peer through the window to see what would happen.

"You think it's doing anything?" she asked after a minute.

"I don't know. How long does it take to heat something in the electric oven?"

Suddenly a little flame appeared. It danced around as the whole thing turned on the plate. Pete opened the door and pulled the corner of the paper until it slid onto the floor. He stomped it with his boot until the fire was out. Then he picked up the wad and held it with two fingers, the charred corner leaving black ash everywhere. He let out a growl as he examined it, his forehead drawn tight. His jaw clenched.

"Sorry, Pete," she said. "Maybe that wasn't the right setting." She wanted to laugh but knew better. When a man was that angry you didn't push him.

His arm went up and Elizabeth instinctively put her hands in front of her with a gasp.

"What's wrong with you?" he asked.

She felt his hand gently pull at her wrist until her hands were down again but her breathing was still heavy.

"I was just scratching my head. Did you think I was going to hit you?" He cocked his head to the side, examining her.

"Of course not." She turned and grabbed a paper towel from the counter and wet it at the sink. Then she dropped to the floor and began wiping away the tiny burned pieces.

"I didn't mean to scare you. Did I really look that angry?"

How was she to explain her behavior? "Nay. You go relax a while. It's your day off, remember? I'll fix you a nice supper. It'll be ready in no time." She pretended the floor was still dirty and rubbed at it until he left the room, throwing the sandwich wad in the trash as he went.

Silent tears began to fall. She hoped Pete didn't tell anyone how she'd acted. Would she always be this way? Afraid of her own shadow? Coming to Asheville was supposed to fix everything, so why was she still so broken?

CHAPTER FIVE

Friday evening, after the men returned from the sawmill, the group loaded into Nathan's car for a "grocery and beer run," as the men called it. Elizabeth wanted to stay at the house, but knew Nathan wouldn't bring home the right things from the grocery list if she did. She wondered where else they planned on going.

The evening before, the men had given each other haircuts, short ones like the men in Asheville wore. Now they looked just like everyone else and so did Rebecca. Elizabeth supposed some of the women wore long skirts like the one she had on, but hardly any of them were her age. She left her hair down and flowing to compensate. None of the women in the community would wear their hair down unless they were going to bed. It often tickled her arm, making her think a spider was crawling on her, but that was nothing compared to getting it caught everywhere. If she wasn't careful she'd shut the car door on it, but she refused to braid it. She wondered why some of the *Ordnung* rules were easy to break, and others were so hard as they neared the busiest part of town.

They stopped at a Mexican restaurant that smelled like pickles, fried cheese, and air conditioning. It had carpet, short and dark, and Elizabeth wondered how they ever kept it clean. A woman showed them to a rounded booth in the corner of the room. The men sat down on one side and Elizabeth and Rebecca took the other. Elizabeth scooted over and found herself sitting next to Nathan. They ordered dishes they couldn't pronounce and snacked on chips and spicy salsa while they waited for their order.

"So," Nathan said. "What do you think of the world outside of the community so far?" He was addressing the whole table.

"I like it," James said and took a long drink of his beer.

"Me too," Rebecca said. "I think I could get used to hot showers and working outside of the kitchen. I may never go home."

"Do you really mean that?" Pete asked.

"Yes," she said.

"I miss some things." Pete laid his arms on the table.

"Like what?" Nathan asked.

"Like...the smell of fresh bread in the morning, some of the people, a quiet room."

Elizabeth watched sweat beads run down her soda glass.

Nathan took a drink of beer. "Well, my *dat* would never allow beer in the house and I have to say I'd miss it if I left."

"Are you thinking about staying permanently?" Elizabeth said before thinking better of it.

He set his beer in front of him. "I don't know. Maybe. What about you?"

The waitress walked up, carrying a large tray. "Do you need another beer, sir?" she asked.

"Yes, please," Nathan said, smiling wide.

She set a plate down in front of each of them and left with Nathan's empty glass.

Elizabeth waited for someone to suggest a moment of prayer over their meal, but no one did. She thought about how to answer Nathan's question should he ask again. She had no intention of ever going home, but she wondered if she should keep that to herself for now. But perhaps if Nathan was thinking on it, then maybe it was okay for her to be, too.

An hour later they entered the Asheville Supercenter. "What do you think," Nathan asked. "Meet back at the car by seven?"

Everyone agreed and went their separate ways except Nathan. He carried the grocery money for the group and would need to pay for all the food they planned on buying for the barbeque tomorrow night. Elizabeth got a grocery cart and pulled the list from her pocket.

"What do we need for the barbeque?" she asked as they began walking down the first aisle.

"I'll get the things for the barbeque, you can shop for everything else. Deal?"

She nodded. "What kind of snacks do you want for this week?" She knew he liked spicy chips, but she wasn't sure what else to buy. Back home they never bought such frivolous things. If you didn't get enough at mealtimes you simply waited until the next meal, but perhaps that wasn't what Nathan and the others were used to.

Nathan picked up a box of cheese crackers and set them in the cart. Elizabeth picked up the box and studied it, the picture on the front bringing back memories. *Mah* had made cheesy crackers from shredded cheese, butter, flour, salt, and cold water, but Elizabeth couldn't remember how much of everything she used. She'd searched the recipe box but couldn't find anything that fit the description, and the other ladies that knew her didn't have it either. Elizabeth remembered her younger sisters always having a small bag of those orange circles during the long church services.

She recalled *Mah* cutting them with a homemade cookie cutter she'd made from a tin can and shaped into a circle no bigger than a quarter.

"Wouldn't it be easier, *Mah*, to make them all square?" she'd asked. Her *mueter* smiled brightly. Elizabeth could barely remember what she looked like now, and with no pictures to refresh her memory it was the image she reached for each time she tried, her *mueter* smiling at her right at that moment.

Then she said, "Sometimes, Elizabeth, you go out of your way to make things extra special for those you love." Then she went about cutting the small circles out of the rolled out dough.

"They're only two dollars, Elizabeth," Nathan said.

"What?" She looked up at Nathan, the box still in her hand. "Oh, right." She set the box down and a woman with two young girls walked by, the *mueter* pushing a cart. She wondered if the girls knew just how lucky they were.

The barbeque had started civil enough. Seven people with the promise of more had unloaded barbeque grills and coolers full of beer. Nathan, Pete, James, and Carlos each watched a grill while the rest of the people drank and socialized. Rebecca looked completely at home, flirting with two *Englisher* men at once. But after the food was ready and everyone had eaten, some of them began acting strangely. Carlos suggested they turn on some music inside the house so the neighbors didn't complain and call the police. He said outside music almost always earned them a visit from the cops and they didn't want that. Lured by the music, many of the guests moved inside. Soon the house was crawling with people.

Elizabeth watched as a girl about her age stumbled twice trying to get to the restroom. Why anyone would allow themselves to act that way in front of others, Elizabeth couldn't guess. A guy was kissing a girl in the corner, and Elizabeth had to ask a girl to please get down from the table before she hurt herself.

Elizabeth bit at her fingernail, imagining the police barging through the door and taking them all to jail. Then the bishop or one of the deacons would be brought in to identify everyone and send them all back to the settlement.

Oh, when will this night end?

Searching for a place to hide until it was over, Elizabeth opened the bedroom door. There lay Rebecca under the covers with Carlos. Elizabeth shut the door fast, her heart beating out of her chest. Her mind raced. Carlos hadn't acted the least bit interested in Rebecca when he'd visited last week. What had changed so dramatically to have them in bed together? She shook her head, trying to rid herself of the image. At least he wouldn't be flirting with Elizabeth anymore.

Was there no order in this house at all? Elizabeth pushed her way through the crowd and out the sliding glass door.

In the back porch light Nathan stood with the other men.

"I thought you had to have a beard to buy beer," James said.

"No, *doomkupf*, you just have to have a license," Pete

corrected him. Pete's eyes met hers. She had been avoiding him since the incident with the microwave. Elizabeth looked away.

"But I can't drive," James said.

"You don't have to drive," Nathan said, holding a beer in his hand. "It's another kind of license."

"What kind?" James asked.

"I don't know. They give them at the license office. You'll have to ask them."

Elizabeth stepped up. "Nathan, things are getting a little out of hand in there. Are you sure the landlord will allow this?"

James's face twisted. "What do they allow you to do if not drive?"

"Just tell them you want a beer license," Pete said.

"No, no, it's not a beer license," Nathan went on. "It's just to see how old you are."

"Nathan," she pleaded. "Please?"

He turned to her, finally acknowledging her presence with wide eyes. "What's wrong?"

"Just take a walk through the house and see what's going on in there." Surely if he saw for himself he would agree things were going too far.

"Sure thing, little lady," he said and walked into the house with steps that weren't entirely steady.

"Are you okay?" Pete eyed her sharply.

"*Ja,* I'm fine." She followed Nathan, stepping inside the door only a few seconds after he'd shut it. She searched the crowd. Where was he?

"Well, hello there, beautiful," a voice came from beside her. "Won't you come sit with me a while." A man, much older than she was, with large biceps bulging from beneath his thin tee-shirt pulled her wrist until they were both sitting on the couch. He put one arm around her and leaned in very close. Did he mean to kiss her? Elizabeth's breath caught.

What do I do?

Should she try to run or scream? Or should she kiss him back? He smelled like gasoline and beer, but he was an attractive man. How did she get in this situation? She didn't even know the man's name. There wasn't time for a decision before his wet lips met hers, his tongue sliding in her mouth along with the sour taste of beer.

Live a little. Nathan's words chanted in her brain. This was what the group expected of her. She was on *Rumspringa* to experiment and she'd never been kissed before.

Rebecca was certainly getting her experimenting in tonight.

Elizabeth began kissing him back, his mouth moving all over hers strangely. Then his other hand moved under her shirt, touching the bare skin of her waist and heading upward. She pulled his hand down. "What are you doing?" she asked, taking in a heavy breath.

"I'm just having a little fun," he said, leaning forward. She leaned far away from him and quickly found herself lying on her back on the couch with the man on top of her. He began kissing her again and she pushed at him with her hands.

"Get off me!" she shouted. Her head turned to the side. There were people everywhere. How far would he go? "Help," she screamed over the music.

"Get off her!" Nathan yelled, dropping his beer can to pull the man away.

"What's the big idea?" the man said.

"Get out." Nathan pointed to the door.

69

The man turned as if headed toward the door then reared back and swung at Nathan. Nathan dodged and grabbed his arm, twisting it until the man winced. "Get out," he said, letting him go. The man gave Nathan the evil eye before he stumbled out of the house without a word.

"Are you all right?" Nathan held out his hand and pulled Elizabeth to her shaking feet.

She pressed her lips together to keep from crying. Around them everyone moved and danced as if nothing happened.

"Come on," he said, pulling her out the sliding glass door by her hand, the music still blaring in her ears.

Outside, James and Pete crowded around. "What's wrong?" Pete asked.

"Some guy tried to assault Elizabeth on the couch." Nathan released her to sit in a lawn chair beside them.

"Where is he?" James asked, smacking his fist into the palm of his other hand.

"He's gone," Nathan said, "but she's shook up."

"Are you okay, Elizabeth?" Pete asked her, squatting down beside her chair to look her in the eye. She nodded her head tightly, straightening her clothes.

Nathan took a deep breath and let it all out at once. "You should probably stick with Rebecca the rest of the night."

She shook her head as the image of Rebecca and Carlos came back to her.

"Why not?"

"I can't say." Elizabeth put her head down.

"Where is she?" Nathan asked.

Silence.

"Answer me," he growled.

"She's in the bedroom with Carlos."

She lifted her head and watched the group exchange glances.

Nathan swallowed hard. "Well, is she...okay?"

"She's where she wants to be, if that's what you're asking. I don't believe anyone who is drinking is actually okay."

James and Pete looked at the beer in their hands.

"She's right, fellas," Nathan said. "It's not a good idea for all these people to be drinking together. Someone has to keep watch."

~

The next day was Sunday. If Elizabeth had remembered her days right, it was a church day. Her *vater* would be taking her two sisters to the Hilty's farm for services in their barn while Elizabeth spent the rest of the morning cleaning up trash and trying to get the smell of spilled beer out of the carpet. She'd worked for a couple of hours already while everyone else slept, cleaning up the kitchen. She wondered what it was about beer that made people act so crazy and then sleep so late.

A noise came from the men's room. They'd be needing coffee of the strongest kind. She stopped what she was doing and made some.

Pete appeared. She had expected Nathan. He was the one who usually woke first.

"*Goota morga,* uh...I mean, good morning. Care for some coffee?" she asked.

"Please."

She placed a hot cup in front of him. "Anyone else awake yet?" she asked.

"*Nay.*" His face was solemn.

"Well, there's plenty to do around here. I've got to get moving." Elizabeth started to walk out of the kitchen.

"You're not going back, are you?" he asked.

The question caught her by surprise. "What do you mean?"

"Deep down I think we all knew we would. Well, I don't know about Rebecca, but the rest of us. But you're different."

Her pulse sped. "I don't know what you're talking about."

"You didn't come for *Rumspringa*. You came to get away from home."

A flash of heat washed over her as she dropped down into the chair beside him and lowered her voice. "Please, Pete. Don't tell the others."

"There's no shame in it, Elizabeth. You don't have to go home to your *vater*, but go home. Don't stay out here. You'll soon be by yourself and you won't have Nathan to protect you."

He was speaking the truth. They would leave and she'd be all alone. But what choice did she have? He didn't know her *vater*. He'd never let her live with anyone else, not before she was married, not even with her aunt in Indiana. All the mean things he'd done to her over the years since her *mueter's* death...

She'd always thought no one would believe her, but now the question was, what if they did? He'd kill her before he'd be shamed that way. Her mind flashed back to the time he had pointed a shotgun at her, and the years that followed had told her she was right to get out of the way.

She smiled tensely. "Thank you, Pete, for being concerned about me, but I'm fine, really."

"I'm just saying this because I'm leaving the house

today. I'm going back home to join church. I've had enough of the *Englisher* life."

She thought a moment. "I'm glad for you, Pete. I wish you all the happiness in the world. Will you tell my sister, Lydia, that I'm okay? I'll get to see her whenever I can."

"What's this about happiness?" Nathan was now in the kitchen pulling up a chair.

"Nothing," she answered quickly, blinking back tears. "Would you care for some coffee?" Elizabeth jumped up and poured him a cup, trying not to meet Pete's eyes, which were boring a hole through her.

CHAPTER SIX

lizabeth sat in a lawn chair under the back porch light watching Nathan sip a can of soda. He continued to host parties with coolers full of beer and allowed James to get completely drunk, but suddenly stopped drinking any himself. Was he changing for the better? She had watched a cute blonde practically sit on his lap to get him to kiss her last weekend, but he'd turned her away because he'd said she wasn't in her right mind. Elizabeth doubted she'd remembered any of it the next day. James never did.

It had been weeks since the man had pinned her down on the couch and Nathan had kept her close during parties since. Could he be growing sweet on her? She wouldn't get her hopes up.

Rebecca pulled along a new fellow Elizabeth had never seen before through the crowd and in through the sliding glass door.

Probably to the bedroom.

How could she forget her upbringing so quickly?

Rebecca came from a *guete* home—at least Elizabeth had always thought she had.

Everyone probably thinks the same about me.

Well, everyone but Pete, but he was back home now. Elizabeth scolded herself for judging Rebecca. What she did was between her and the Lord and none of anyone's business. She, too, had many sins to be sorry for.

She thought back to what Pete had said about everyone leaving her at some point. It had nagged at her ever since. It was time for her to get a job and stand on her own.

"Nathan, do you think there's anything for me to do down at the sawmill?"

"The sawmill is man's work, Elizabeth. Besides, you do a great job keeping house for us. You don't need to work."

She forgot she already had a job. Nathan wouldn't let her work. She would have to wait until he went home first.

Twisting in her chair she said, "Are we just going to sit here?"

Each weekend they hung out and waited for everyone to get too drunk to walk and then Nathan would send them all home. Then the next morning they would all work together to clean up, if Elizabeth hadn't finished before they got out of bed.

"What do you mean?" he asked. "Aren't you having fun?"

"*Nay,* are you?"

He thought a moment. "I guess not. What do you suggest?"

"You don't have to babysit me, Nathan. You can go have fun with your friends if you want." She waited to see if he would go or not. Had he grown up since moving to Asheville? She sighed. Anything was preferable to just sitting and doing nothing. He wasn't even making conversation.

"If something happened to you or Rebecca in this house I'd be responsible. I shouldn't have brought either one of you along."

His words cut her heart like a knife. In the time they'd spent together, did she still mean nothing to him? She nodded her head slowly, her face filling with heat. She stood to her feet.

"I didn't mean it like that, Elizabeth."

She stomped to the door and as soon as it opened the music came blaring out. James staggered around the middle of the room, trying to dance. He fell to the floor. The crowd around him laughed. "Get back up," they yelled. James was shouting in Swiss German—not nice things—but she doubted anyone else knew what he was saying.

Unable to find a quieter place in the house, Elizabeth locked herself in the restroom until someone banged on it about twenty minutes later.

Outside the door, Nathan stood kissing a brunette with a stick figure and a lot of skin showing. She slipped past him and back outside. What was she doing here? If the others were going to leave eventually anyway she may as well go now. She could get a job by the end of the week and maybe be able to afford her own place before they went back home. She certainly didn't want to stay and watch her friends destroy themselves anymore.

She leaned over the porch rail, cleansing herself with the cool night air.

A warm arm wrapped around her.

"Nathan, I..." But it wasn't Nathan. It was the same man who had held her down before. She gasped. "You!" she shouted in surprise. All the blood drained from her face and ran down to her toes.

Why had she left Nathan?

He'd never hear her out here.

"You remember me?" he asked. "I've been thinking about the way you kissed me ever since we met." He leaned toward her.

"We never actually met, really." She pushed him back with her hands.

"I'm Butch. You got a name, sweetheart?" He pushed his face into her neck, hot breath and prickly whiskers made her body tremble. Nothing short of Nathan's fist was going to stop this guy and like a *doomkupf* she'd ran away from him.

"Get away from me or I'll..."

"You'll what?" he said, stopping only for a brief second to ask. He tugged at the collar of her shirt.

Her jaw dropped open but Butch covered her mouth. She bit his hand, hard. He let out a curse word and released her.

She lunged past him. Heavy hands grabbed her around the waist. She screamed, clawing at his arms. The sliding glass door opened and a man stepped out holding a can of beer.

"Help me!" she yelled.

The man staggered over to Butch and said, "What's going on over here?"

She screamed again and the man put his free hand over his ear.

"She's a loud one, ain't she?" he said.

"Yeah," Butch said, "she's my wife."

His wife?

She screamed again. "Let me go!"

"Elizabeth?" Nathan appeared behind the man.

"Nathan, help!"

She ducked and Nathan planted a fist in the man's face.

Butch fell to the ground, almost taking Elizabeth down with him. When he didn't get up, Nathan took Elizabeth by the hand and led her through the house, ordering everyone out.

The party was over.

~

Hot coffee steamed in the tin cup. It had to be Nathan Elizabeth heard stirring. James would probably sleep till noon or later, and Rebecca was never up before ten on a Sunday. She set the cup at his place at the table then poured herself some, enjoying the aroma more than the hot drink.

Nathan entered the room with a sagging face and half-opened eyes. "No more parties," he said simply and sat down in front of his coffee. Elizabeth did her best to keep a straight face. He had finally seen what she had all along.

"I'm sorry I ruined your *Rumspringa*," she said before taking a sip of her coffee.

"*Rumspringa's* not over yet. We just have to do things differently."

She sighed, fighting the urge to roll her eyes. No matter. She would be getting a job—hopefully tomorrow.

Nathan helped her clean up the house, removing the trash and cleaning the floors and yard. When they were finished, both the other housemates were still asleep.

"Do you want to go out for breakfast? We could bring back something for the others," Nathan said.

"Sure, I'd like that."

They left a note, got in Nathan's car, and headed down the street toward a little *café*. Inside, Elizabeth was taken back to a time she had visited the restaurant with her *Mah*.

"You're sure this is the same *café*?" Nathan asked.

78

"*Ja.* I think we sat over there, by the window."

They sat down and a waitress gave them each a menu.

They looked over it in silence until the woman returned a moment later.

"What happened to her?" he asked after the waitress took their order and disappeared into the back.

"She died of cancer."

"What kind?"

"I don't remember and it's not spoken of. I just remember it was only a few weeks after she went to the doctor."

"That must have been hard on you girls. Your *vater* never remarried, did he?"

"*Nay.*" She hoped he didn't ask why. Her theory wasn't for nice company.

"He must have loved her very much."

She nodded. He did. That was one thing she could say about *Dah.* He loved *Mah* more than anything. He was a jealous man, too. He didn't even want anyone looking in her direction. She would have pitied the man who'd tried to handle her *mah* the way Butch had her. *Dah* would have torn him in half.

"What about you?" she asked. "What's your family like?"

He filed through the sugar packets, pushing them back and forth in the small, white container on the table. "They're...perfect."

"You say that like it's a bad thing."

"*Nay*, it's not that. I love them very much. I just want to let loose a while, you know? No one in my family has ever went away for *Rumspringa* and I wanted to be the first."

"Have you made a name for yourself yet?" She raised her eyebrows in question.

79

He shook his head. "I didn't mean it pridefully. It's hard to explain. You're the oldest. Don't you understand the feeling that it's all on you?"

"I do."

"I'm sorry, Elizabeth. I know you had it much differently. I'm sorry I said anything."

"So what should we bring back for the others?" she said, changing the subject.

He looked deep into her eyes. "I'm not worried about the others."

Heat rose in Elizabeth's cheeks. She pondered what he meant by the statement all through breakfast.

Afterward, as Nathan paid the bill up front, she spied a blackbird made of resin in a display case below the cash register. She squatted down to see it better.

"What is it?" he asked.

"Nothing," she said, not taking her eyes off it.

"Could we see the bird in the case?" he asked the lady.

She pulled it out and set it on top of the glass counter. It was a perfect likeness of a crow with its head cocked slightly to the side, a perfect match to the real thing.

"It's beautiful," she said.

"We'll take it." Nathan pulled out some money from his billfold and handed it to the lady.

"Oh, no, I couldn't."

"Sure you can."

"I couldn't keep it."

"You mean when you return? That would be up to you. The bishop doesn't have to know everything."

Elizabeth gasped.

A smile spread across his lips. "Keep it as long as you're comfortable, is what I meant."

She held the bird in her hands as if it were alive and

WHAT HAPPENS IN ASHEVILLE

might fly away. Tears formed in her eyes at the memory of the birds she'd once loved.

"Are you okay?" He leaned over, staring directly in her face.

She turned away from him. "*Ja*, I think I just got something in my eye."

"You're a poor liar, Elizabeth." He laughed as they started for the car.

When they arrived, Elizabeth remembered how they were going to get breakfast for everyone. "I can make something up," she said, shutting the car door.

"I should have remembered. I can help." Nathan stopped. "Do you hear that?"

"Horse hooves," she said.

They turned around. A horse and buggy approached and stopped in front of the house. It was Pete, dressed plain once again. "Is James here?" he shouted.

"I think so," Nathan said, "what's wrong?"

"It's *Dat*. He's had a heart attack. I've come to fetch him."

They ran inside and Pete gave James the news. James hurried into the bedroom and came back a moment later tugging on his suspenders. He plopped his hat on his head.

"What's going on?" Rebecca asked as she came into the room.

Pete told her and she said, "I'm coming, too."

"What?" Elizabeth knew this would happen but she didn't expect it to be so soon.

"I'll be right back," Rebecca said, disappearing into her bedroom and returning with a bag of things.

How did she pack so quickly?

They rushed out the door and were gone as soon as Pete could get the horse turned back the other way.

"I hope their *dah* is okay," Elizabeth said from the driveway as she and Nathan watched them disappear.

"Yeah, me too."

Elizabeth's eyes grew wide. They were alone in the house together. "What about you? Are you going home?" she asked.

"No. But I think you should."

"What?"

"It's not appropriate for us to be here alone together and you know it." Nathan walked back into the house, not waiting for a response.

She followed quickly behind. "Nothing about this trip has been appropriate. What's your point?"

"The point is, it's time for you to go back home and be with your family." He plopped down on the couch.

"And what about you?" She sat down at the other end of the couch and crossed her arms in front of her.

"I'm going to stay around a little while."

"And I will too," she said defiantly.

He sighed. "Okay."

"Okay?" It wasn't like him to give up that easily. She narrowed her eyes at him.

He got up and went out the sliding glass door into the back yard.

Elizabeth went into the restroom. In the trash can beside the toilet was an empty box. She peered at it curiously. A pregnancy test. Her heart sank. So that was why her roommate went home so suddenly. She prayed for her, that her family would forgive and accept her back anyway. If not for her sake, then for the *booplie*.

Just as she was about to start dinner, Nathan came back in the house. "Come on, I'll take you out for lunch."

"Where to?" she asked.

"Anywhere. You've cooked enough."

"That's really nice of you, Nathan, but I don't mind cooking."

"I said I was taking you to lunch, and I'm taking you to lunch. Now, let's go."

His tone was neither mean, nor friendly. Was he still upset with her about not going home?

She'd never rode in the front seat of his car before. They had always traveled with at least one of the others. Elizabeth sat up straight admiring the view. Was it vain that she felt more important riding up front? Perhaps Nathan would see her as more important, too. She let one of her hands feel the breeze through the open window.

"So where are we going?" she asked. They had driven almost all the way across town already and soon there wouldn't be a restaurant left, only the settlement was this far...

"Nathan, no!" she cried. "Please, no."

"It's for your own *guete*, Elizabeth." He didn't turn his head toward her when he spoke.

"You didn't even let me get my things! I can't go home in clothes like these. My bird!"

"I'll bring you all your things another day. The important thing right now is to get you home. You've got to be missing your family and you knew we weren't going to stay in Asheville forever."

"I'm not going home. I'm going to be an *Englisher*," she shouted, tears forming.

"No, you're not and we both know it."

"You don't understand what you're doing." She bit her quivering bottom lip, her insides shaking now. She couldn't go home. Not ever. "Please, Nathan." But no matter how much she pleaded he didn't speak the rest of the way home.

83

It was almost dinnertime when they arrived. She'd been gone a matter of weeks but it felt like a lifetime ago. The sick feeling in her stomach returned. What would *Dah* do to her?

Nathan stopped the car.

She pleaded once more. "Please," she said in a calm, quiet voice, "please, don't leave me here." Elizabeth blinked and a tear splashed on her leg. She hoped he'd understand.

"One day you'll thank me."

She got out and watched him leave in a cloud of dust.

Lydia met her at the door. "*Schweshta*, is that you?"

Elizabeth nodded her head.

Lydia's eyes grew as big as saucers. "You can't be here when *Dah* gets back. Especially looking like that. He's powerful angry with you."

Relief flooded. "You mean he's not here?"

"*Nay*, but he'll be back any minute. What are you going to do?"

Her heart threatened to beat out of her chest. "Where is he? Do you know?"

"I think he's in the north field."

"I'll walk back to town."

"It's ten miles to town!" She held her stare in a moment of understanding then touched Elizabeth's long blonde hair. "Take some rolls from the table and I'll get you a glass of water."

They ran inside and Lydia quickly filled a pint jar and capped it with a canning lid and ring. She handed it to her along with a sack for her dinner rolls. Elizabeth gave her a hug. "*Danki, schweshta.*"

"God be with you," she said, nearly pushing her out the door.

Elizabeth hurried down the drive, gravel crunching

beneath her feet as she dropped the jar into the sack along with the rolls. No one could see her dressed like this, especially not her *vater*. A crow cried out from above, and her feet moved even faster.

~

It was past suppertime when Elizabeth arrived back at the rental house with sore feet and a tingling in her legs. After rehearsing for hours what she would say, she stood at the door with nothing. She took a deep breath and walked in. She'd just tell him the truth. That she wasn't going home and she wasn't taking no for an answer. She would get a job and if he would just please let her stay until she found a new place to live that would be much appreciated. She smiled at herself for coming up with that last minute.

Then she smelled smoke. Rushing into the kitchen, she found Nathan with a flaming skillet standing at the stove. Elizabeth ran to the cabinet and pulled out the lid and quickly set it on top. Then she turned off the burner and took the handle, carrying it carefully over to the sink.

"I could have done that." Nathan put his hands on his hips.

"Sure you could of," she said. Then she went to her room and shut the door. She was much too tired to eat and she figured morning would make a better time to chat with Nathan anyway.

~

"I'm getting a job," Elizabeth said as Nathan took his first sip of coffee the next morning before work. "And I'm moving out as soon as I have the money. I know you don't want me here and that's fine. I'll do my best to stay out of your way and let you continue your *Rumspringa*. Don't do me any more favors, Nathan. What I do is my own business. Now, do you want breakfast or not?"

"How did you get back here yesterday?" he asked.

"I walked."

"Ten miles?" He raised his eyebrows and leaned back in his chair.

"You'd of had to explain to the landlord how you burned his house down if I hadn't."

He laughed. "All right. You got me. I can't cook."

Elizabeth took out a skillet to start breakfast.

"Ten miles?" he whispered to himself.

Elizabeth gritted her teeth as she cracked the eggs into the skillet. She hadn't thought of herself as tough for walking ten miles back to town, especially since she had no other choice, but if she was going to make it as an *Englisher*, she was going to have to learn to stand up for herself and stop letting people like Nathan Graber push her around. She wasn't going home, not now, not ever.

ABOUT THE AUTHOR

Tattie Maggard lives near Swan Creek, just south of a Swiss Amish community in rural Missouri with her husband, daughter, and three rescue dogs. When she's not chasing black bears from her yard, she's writing Amish romance, homeschooling her daughter, or playing an old tune on the ukulele.

Sign up for Tattie's newsletter for updates and to get a free short story, Mending The Heart, sent straight to your inbox. Visit www.TattieMaggard.com for more info.

Thank you for reading and reviewing. God bless!

 facebook.com/TattieMaggard

 instagram.com/tattiemaggard

ALSO BY TATTIE MAGGARD

The Amish of Swan Creek

A Swiss Amish Christmas

Forbidden Amish Love

An Amish Rumspringa

The Amish Flower Shop

An Amish Heart

Amish Neighbors

Made in the USA
Monee, IL
01 March 2020

22563225R00056